SHAPE AND SHADOWS

THE MISTS OF ELISTA TRILOGY, BOOK 2

CLARA WILS

Gryphon's Gate Publishing

Shape and Shadows

Copyright © 2022 Clara Wils

Gryphon's Gate Publishing

550 King St. N.

PO Box 42088 Conestoga

Waterloo, ON

N2L 6K5

ISBN: 978-1-988115-99-3

Print ISBN: 978-1-990587-00-9

CHAPTER 1

L ATE WINTER IN THE SOUTH OF E LISTA COULD BE QUITE MILD, especially when a warm southeasterly wind swept up off Dyren's Bay. This morning, that pleasant breeze tousled my hair as I stood atop a low seaside cliff, gazing out at a small fleet of ships weighing anchor off the coast.

Fifteen ships, each teeming with hundreds of men, was not a comforting sight first thing in the morning.

"So many," I whispered.

No one around me replied. But I needed someone to say something, needed some reassurance.

"Someone tell me this is going to work," I pleaded with my companions. The sun, pulling higher into the sky, warmed me just a bit more than was comfortable, since I still wore a layer of bandages over most of my body under my clothes.

Maverick grunted, non-committal. I could tell he didn't like this sight at all. He could do little to stop such a force from walking over him and taking these lands.

"Yes, it will work," Alvere, Prince of Vauphan, said beside me. There was something in the quick look and the flash of a smile — perhaps it was the clear depths of his blue eyes — that warmed me just a bit more than the sun did.

I returned his smile, just as the wind blew my brown hair across my face in a mess of wavy curls.

"It better," Amber said. She was still tense and uneasy — also probably exhausted — after tending to the extensive wounds on Ant, her sometimes lover. It was a miracle he was alive. He was a lot tougher than he looked, and he looked massively tough to begin with. He had the ability to heal himself and others, but he needed to be conscious, and he'd been delirious this past day, weak as a kitten.

Fin, the heavy-set yet surprisingly light-on-his-feet senior member of Maverick House was also with us. He'd be needed for his ability to transport himself — and anyone touching him — to any place he'd been before. If this all went well, he'd be going back with the Vauphani troops to set up a route to their palace so the prince could go back and forth with ease.

But first, the five of us had to convince thousands of enemy troops to go home peacefully.

The first ships were disgorging longboats, sending troops ashore.

"Shall we go down then?" the prince asked.

Maverick grunted again, nodding. He led the way down a steep path to the beach. The prince and I came next, with Amber behind us and Fin last.

"He doesn't say much, does he?" Alvere whispered to me, indicating Maverick.

"He can. I think he's just got other things on his mind right now, like surviving this morning."

The prince nodded at that and sighed. I hadn't known the man long, but his expressions and body language seemed easy to read. His current look: tight-lipped, back rigid, eyes a bit distant, seemed to say: *I didn't want any of this, but all of you forced my hand*. Then with a long inhalation, he stood a little taller, chest out, shoulder's back but relaxed, a hard smile on his lips. This look seemed to say: *time to take control*.

A part of me wanted to reach out and take his hand, tell him all would be well, but I didn't. And in truth, I should have been more worried for myself. To the army below, he was their prince, an ally. I was the enemy.

"This will work," he whispered. It seemed mostly to himself, so I didn't say anything.

The rough path down the bluff gave way to a sandy beach. My boots sunk into the shifting grains.

My emotions may have been turbulent and uncertain, but physically I felt surprisingly well. I should have been exhausted and in pain. Two days ago, I'd been shredded — and nearly killed — by The Mistweaver, Hazra. The same madwoman who'd killed Alvere's parents, the king and queen of Vauphan. Ant had healed me a little that night, before he'd gotten *himself* beaten to The Pits, but I'd been healing on my own since then. Also, I'd had trouble sleeping this past day. I'd dozed a little, sleeping for a few hours at a time through the past day and night. Yet, somehow, I wasn't particularly weary or sore.

I think it's your spirit-gift, Auwei said. Auwei was the Lumani spirit who dwelled within me. Our bond allowed me to shape-shift into a spider, my avatar form. I could also use other spider-based abilities in my human form, like walk on walls and spin silk... from my belly button of all places.

Oh? I was curious to hear more. A spirit-gift was a rare additional power that only some True-Bonded — the pairing of human and Lumani — possessed. Maverick could summon fire, Amber could instill simple commands in people's minds, Fin could teleport, Ant could heal.

I've had many hosts, Auwei said. I was her tenth True-Bonded. She'd lived nine lifetimes bonded to others before me. *And none have had your stamina and energy. I think you... I don't know how to put it exactly, but I think your sheer determination and drive has turned into a spirit-gift that allows you to keep going no matter what. I don't know what you'd call that, but Legs, you should be laid up, fatigued and healing, yet you're not. Something special is going on. I believe it is your spirit-gift.*

It would explain a lot. Remembering our escape from the palace of Vauphan, there seemed far too much I'd done that shouldn't have been possible. I'd been thoroughly thrashed by the mistweaver and near death. The only reason I'd survived at all was because Ant had healed me. But he'd only healed my major wounds. After that, I should have been a weak and quivering mess. Yet, I'd subdued the prince — that was when I'd discovered that kissing someone without passion in my heart meant I poisoned them — then managed to lower him carefully down the cliffs on my spider-silk, somehow supporting his weight. And since then, I hadn't slept much, even if I had been taking it easy. I should have been exhausted, but here I was.

You might be right.

We spread out on the beach, two of us to either side of the prince, but keeping our distance, hands out, making it clear we had no weapons.

The first men ashore looked us over, and luckily one of them recognized the prince.

"My prince?" the man said, rushing from the boat, drawing a slender rapier. He had a shock of blond hair and a rather prominent nose.

"It is well, Philipe, put your weapon away, these are not our enemies."

"But Your Highness! The palace, your parents. Have you seen what they did? They declared war upon us and—"

"That is enough, Philipe!" the prince said with stern clarity, though he did not raise his voice.

"Yes, Your Highness."

"Who commands this force?" the prince asked.

"General Hugo de Lanace, Your Highness."

"I know him. Spare these people their lives until I have spoken with him, will you do that? They have been nothing but kind to me." The prince glanced at me from the side of his eye with a faint look which said: *mostly*. The fact that that look had come my way meant he was still a little upset I'd accidentally paralyzed him.

That was fair.

I tried not to get too tense as more and more soldiers landed on the beach, forming up into a small army. The one Alvere had spoken to, Philipe, sent a messenger back to one of the ships, then left to organize some men. I guessed he was an officer.

Needless to say, Amber drew a lot of attention. She couldn't go out dressed in anything less than something spectacular. Today's choice was skin-tight, bright-red, silken pants, the sides of which were made of loose lace, which showed off her tanned skin beneath. On top she wore a white blouse, which I'd first thought was mostly unbuttoned but came to realize didn't have buttons at all on the top half, the plunging collar showing lots of skin.

She smiled and winked at the men on the beach.

I don't think I'd ever felt as confident and cool as Amber looked in that moment. I wore a simple dress with a long skirt and sleeves and no exposed mid-section. I didn't want people to see my bandages. And the point of this meeting wasn't to fight, so I wasn't worried about not having my spider-silk available.

Maverick was in tight buckskin pants and a green shirt, which brought out a little bit of green in his hazel-brown eyes.

Fin, big and imposing, but otherwise a jovial fellow, stood at ease. He wore a loose, long, white shirt and grey pants. I could see a few wary glances in his direction, but the soldiers needn't have worried. He wasn't much of a warrior.

A man in a navy-blue uniform — a shade or two darker than the sapphire attire of the other soldiers — came ashore and went to Philipe. They spoke with haste, then the new man marched over to us, speaking to the prince.

"Your Highness, we feared the worst for you. I am glad to see you well." He eyed the rest of us. "Are these allies? Here to help us seize the lands of the traitorous Elistans?"

"There will be no seizing of lands, general."

The general was tall, with a rigid stance and significant grey at his temples and through most of his beard. This was a man who'd lived a long life and seen a lot of military action. He smiled a bit condescendingly at the prince. "Your Highness—"

"Majesty," Alvere said sharply.

The general blinked. "Sire?"

"My parents are dead, are they not? I have not been crowned, but I am king-to-be."

"Yes, of course Your High— Your Majesty. Now, as to matters of war—"

"You will do as I direct," Alvere finished. "And there will be no war in the *south* of Elista"

The general bristled a little but nodded. "As Your... Majesty commands. Shall we run home like whipped pups with no spoils then? After these Elistans murdered your mother and father in cold blood?"

"What we shall do, General, is sail north and re-enforce our troops massing for battle. That is where the fight shall be. We'll take back our lands and nothing more. And—" Alvere said, seeing another comment coming from the general. "As for the horrible atrocities done at the palace, the person responsible for that is dead." He then motioned to us. "These others believe in our cause, even though they are Elistans. They saved me from the murderess that night. They were trying to stop the woman. They will also be following up inquiries here, so that we can find out who was behind the attack and ensure they are punished."

Alvere then leaned in and put on a bit of a just-between-you-an-me tone. "These Elistans are divided and uncertain. They will be easy to defeat in the North, on our own land, but if we seized lands here in the south, they would be hard to keep. Our supply lines over water would be open to attacks, and their capital is only two days' march from here. We'd be overrun quick enough. We are not brutes and barbarians. We will take back what is ours and see that the right people are punished for the attacks on our soil, but nothing more. We are Vauphani, and we will stand proud on our morals."

The general nodded, chastised and yet somehow also emboldened. "You are right, of course, Your Majesty. I mistook your youth for inexperience, but I see now I was wrong. Forgive me."

"You're forgiven, general. Now please, get these men back on the ships. Myself and one of the Elistans will require passage back to the capital. These others—" again with a motion to us, "—are our allies and will be helping us by rooting out the traitor in their own government. We will need to keep in contact with them. I may be returning here frequently and for long periods to coordinate with them directly."

"I'll arrange for some men to accompany you, for your safety," the general said, and I didn't think he'd give on that point.

"I assure you I will be safe, but will allow a small guard, yes." He looked at Maverick who shrugged and nodded.

"Then it's settled. Let's board the ships and be on our way," Alvere finished.

"Back to the ships, men!" the general called out. Those who'd already come ashore began heading back to the boats.

"I'll return once I'm set at home," Alvere said to us. He took a step toward Maverick and whispered. "And I'll make sure your man is returned to you, if we have him."

Maverick gave a terse nod.

Instantly I felt like I'd been punched in the gut.

Silence!

I'd not thought of him since the mention of war, yet... the prince had. How could I have forgotten someone so dear to me? A friend and lover. The one I'd known the longest. The one who'd been with me back at Silverveil and helped to save my life! How could I have forgotten him, even if only for a moment?

"I'll see you all soon," Alvere said. He turned his jewel-blue eyes — like clear, dark beryl — to me. I can't say how I must have looked in that moment, but his brow furrowed, darkening. He nodded to me, then looked to Fin. The large man nodded and the two of them made their way down to the boats.

The rest of us retreated up the beach, to the path up the cliff.

As we reached the waving grasses at the top of the bluff, Amber put a comforting arm around me. "It happens to all of us."

I leaned into her for a moment. She was surprisingly strong, pulling me close to her side as we walked.

"How did you know?" I asked softly.

"It wasn't hard to guess. You looked like someone had crushed your heart when the prince mentioned 'our man.'"

I looked ahead at Maverick, walking stoically, still tall and strong. "How does he do it? It seems like he doesn't care, but I know he does."

"That, child, I have no clue. He's always been like that." She drew in a breath, squeezing me close, then releasing me to walk on my own. "Did anyone ever tell you where he got his spirit-gift from?"

"No." Ant had mentioned some theories on where our crew's spirit-gifts had come from. He'd told me Amber could control people's minds because she wished more than anything to be all anyone thought about.

But as for Maverick's fire...?

"Midnight told me once. She believes his powers come from being hot and cold at the same time. Did you know he could summon cold too?"

I shook my head. That was news to me.

We reached the carriage which had brought us to the coast. Amber and I got in while Maverick joined the driver up front. Soon, we were headed back along the rough road to Hedgewild Manor.

Out the window I saw farmer's fields, newly tilled and waiting for spring crops.

Amber continued her explanation of Maverick's gift; voice hushed a little. "Sometimes, when he can't do anything about a situation, he gets cold. Also, if he's truly furious, a cold anger, then the temperature around him drops. That's the scariest thing I've ever experienced." She drew in a breath then let it out in a bit of a laugh. "I guess you could say he runs hot and cold? Anyway, Midnight thinks this strange ability comes from how much he cares for his family, us, his House. He's fiercely close and warm, but sometimes he cares so much that he also becomes distant. I know that sounds odd, but essentially, at times like this, he can't be thinking about what might have happened to Silence. He can't help the man, he can't be fire, so he's ice instead, unfeeling, except toward the rest of us, for whom he's warm. It's... an odd combination, but it works for him."

I think I understood the man a little better now. Amber was always a font of interesting information.

"I'm... I'm sure Silence will be well," she said a bit haltingly, not as reassuring as I think she'd hoped to be.

I nodded, but said nothing. I still felt a little hollow, and I'd continue to feel this way until I knew Silence was safe.

I wouldn't allow myself to forget him again.

CHAPTER 2

I FRETTED FOR ANOTHER DAY. ONCE AGAIN, I SLEPT periodically, and generally not in my bed. I dozed off once in the library with a book — that I wasn't reading — in my lap. Later, I fell asleep with my head on my arms, slumped over a table in the great hall, an untouched cup of tea next to me.

The only thing of note I did that day was check my bandages. Well, Crane did. She removed the old ones and bathed me with a sponge, cleaning the wounds, but we were both a little shocked at what few injuries remained.

"I hate to doubt the word of Lord Maverick, but the wounds he described upon you... he must have been exaggerating."

I sighed. "No, he wasn't. Auwei thinks I'm developing a spirit-gift."

Crane blinked at that. "So young? Around healing?" She was a bit taken aback.

"Not healing so much as... keeping going. Doing whatever it takes to move past what's hurting me and do what I need to do. It's hard to put into words, but it's the only way to explain this." I motioned to my body. "I should be far more injured."

Crane nodded. "Auwei may be right. Now that I look closer, I can see the scars of the other wounds. By-The-Spirits there are a lot. And... nearly all healed up now. Amazing!"

I shrugged at the off-handed compliment.

We bandaged my right thigh, left calf, and left upper arm. Those were the only places with significant wounds still showing.

"You should tell Lord Maverick about your spirit-gift," Crane said as she left with the bundle of soiled bandages. "He has a way of discerning a person's gift, sometimes even before they do."

I nodded. "I will, thank you."

I went to see Maverick next, hoping that might take up some of this dreadful time waiting. He wasn't in the house. Sparrow, studiously reading in the library, told me he was probably out in the back pasture.

That shocked me a little.

I wandered out into the fields behind the estate as the day waned. The sun was dropping toward the west. It would be dinnertime soon.

I saw a large lone bull grazing in an open field. An actual bull would have been in an enclosure. Still, I didn't approach right away. I'd never seen Maverick in his avatar form before, and he was quite the sight. He was a bull of a man, but this was something else entirely. The heavy body, thickly muscled... everywhere, that heavy head with long horns. I'd thought him imposing as a man, even if he wasn't as big as Ant or Fin, he had a quiet power about him... and now I knew why. The thought of that massive bull charging me, sent chills through me.

He's impressive as man or beast, Auwei commented.

"Maverick?" I called out as I tentatively approached.

That large, heavy head swung in my direction and a moment later it was the man standing before me, latent power in his easy stance.

"Legs?" He crossed the distance between us with a few long strides and gently enfolded me in his arms. "I know. I hate waiting too."

I tried not to cry, though I think a tear did escape one of my eyes. The earthy musk and latent heat of Maverick's body soothed me. I'd never felt such nurturing warmth from another person, even my foster parents. They'd hugged me, but never like this, never so intensely. After a moment, I sighed, feeling much better than I had when I'd come out here. I also remembered *why* I'd come.

"Auwei thinks I might have a spirit-gift," I confided. "And Crane said you're good at figuring out things like that."

A deep and rumbling chuckle emanated from that thick chest. "Yes, it is one of the few things I'm good at." He released me, stepping back, but keeping his hands on my shoulders. He looked me over, eyes narrowed. After a moment of this, he drew in a breath. "Yes, there is something there. It's new and budding still, but there's something. Tell me what effects you've been seeing, and I'll see if I can't divine your spirit-gift."

He motioned to a patch of grass, sitting himself down cross-legged. I did the same, hands resting in my lap. "Well..." I pushed one hand up the loose sleeve of my dress, revealing the unbandaged arm. "I seem to heal quickly. I... I don't know, but I suspect I can't heal others though, like Ant does."

Maverick nodded. "Go on."

"Well, I told you some of what happened when we were

escaping the palace, but I didn't really tell you..." *Any idea how to describe this*? I asked Auwei.

You did things you shouldn't have been able to do. You pushed through and past exhaustion and pain and fear and showed strength far beyond what should have been possible.

You make me sound super-human when you say it that way.

You have a glowing ball of energy residing inside you and possess powers of a spider already. You were superhuman to begin with. This is even more.

Right...

I relayed what Auwei had said.

Maverick's brows rose.

"To be specific... well... you saw what state I was in when I got back, but still, somehow I managed to find the strength to lower the prince down a three-hundred-foot cliff on my spider silk. I kept thinking I couldn't do it, that I'd drop him, but... I didn't." I shrugged.

Maverick nodded.

He seemed to look within me again, and asked: "Auwei... why did you Choose Legs?"

This would be interesting. I stilled my body and let her take over, so she could respond. Her spirit bubbled up to fill me and I heard and felt her speaking through my lips. "At first... I saw just an ordinary girl, but then... there was a flash of something: a spirit and energy that called me back to her. I have sensed it on and off. She is... so determined and driven. She wanted to be a Noble, even though she didn't know quite why. But I think it's because she's driven to stop people from hurting others."

I smiled at that, as Auwei retreated within me.

Maverick drew in a long breath. "I'm guessing Ant told you where spirit-gifts come from?" he asked but didn't wait for an answer. "They come from what we love, what we need." He looked away. "Ant needs to ease the pain of others. Amber needs to be in control. Fin needs to see all the wonderous places of this world. I... I need... to kindle a fire in others, while remaining cool myself." He shrugged. "That's the best way I can describe it." He looked at me for a long moment. "What do you think you love, Legs? What do you need most in this world?"

I thought about that for a moment, considering Auwei's words.

"I can't abide bullies. I need to help those who can't help themselves?" I hadn't meant for it to be a question. "I love... helping?"

He laughed a little. "No Legs... it's a bit more than that."

He observed me intently as he went on. "Yes, you need to help, to defend, to stand up to those who would push others around, but I think what you love most isn't so much the helping part, as the feeling you get once you've helped, when you've put a bully in their place."

He nodded to himself as if he'd reached some conclusion. "You, Legs, need to be a hero." Another breath of a laugh. "And I should have seen it sooner, especially given what we heard from that mistweaver. They saw the future. We know you're going to disrupt the plans of the Nobles behind all of this. You couldn't *not* do it. It's in your blood. They're bullies, and you'll stop them at any cost." He sighed heavily. "You're going to be a handful for... anyone and everyone in your life. You're always going to be running toward danger, not away."

His words made my heart constrict a little, remembering how terrified I'd been in the King's Hall at Vauphan. I hadn't helped the king and queen. I'd been too afraid. "Then... why was I so afraid to help initially when the mistweaver attacked?" I asked, throat closing up, voice tight, as tears came to my eyes. "I... couldn't do anything but cower."

"And what made you stop cowering? What made you fight?" he asked softly.

My chest seized up even more at the thought. "Silence," I could barely say his name. I may have saved him from the mistweaver, but I was the one who'd told him to run off with the news of the war with Vauphan. If I hadn't, then he would have stayed with Amber and...

"You saved him." Maverick's tone was calming. I looked up through bleary eyes, blinking my tears away. They fled down my cheeks as I tried to get myself under control. "So, just to make sure I'm hearing this right: you didn't want to take on one of the most powerful beings in the world at first? But then... you decided you would, to help a friend. For one friend, you'd take on a mistweaver. Legs, there is no shame in running or hiding from a superior foe. That's what most of us sane people would do."

He reached out to lay a hand on my knee. "But you couldn't flee with Silence, could you? You wanted to protect him and fight against that superior foe." Maverick nodded to himself. "If I had to make a guess, I'd say that's when your spirit-gift blossomed."

He lowered his voice a little, a conspiratorial tone. "Something tells me you won't be hiding or running away much anymore. I don't think you'll be able to." A heavy sigh. "And your gift is going to allow you to do that. It will heal you and give you strength to fight those fights." He shook his head slowly. "And it's only going to get stronger. Assuming you live long enough, you could become one of the most powerful True-Bonded ever."

I didn't feel strong right now.

Maverick rose and offered his hand to help me up. I took

it and once again found myself in his arms, surrounded by his tender warmth. "Your life is probably going to be riddled with pain and loss, Legs, but it will also make you a force to be reckoned with." I felt his heavy sigh. "Come on, let's go in and wait for the prince to return."

He released me and we walked back to the house together.

"So…" he said conversationally. "What do you think of the prince?"

"He seems like a kind and proper man."

"He certainly is handsome, with those stunning blue eyes."

"Well, yes, I suppose so." I felt myself flush a little, remembering some of the private looks the prince had sent my way. "I certainly think—" I stopped myself, looking up at Maverick. "*You* think he's handsome?"

No Legs, he was goading you on a little. He's apparently seen the way you look at the prince.

Oh? And how do I look at the prince?

The same way he looks at you… with… interest.

I am not interested in him, I love Silence. But even as I thought those words, I questioned them. I didn't question my love for Silence, more… I questioned whether I wished to love *only* Silence. I'd felt for some time that I wanted more, but that I wouldn't risk what I had with Silence to get it. I wanted him to want more too. I'd asked him about that, the last night we were together and he'd not been able to answer me.

The prince was handsome and did seem interested. A part of me was curious too, according to Auwei. But I wouldn't betray Silence. I'd wait for his answer to me… and hope he wanted what I wanted.

Maverick laughed lightly, a friendly thing. "Someday

you're going to figure yourself out, and when you do... oh, watch out world."

Figure myself out?

You are more than a little tied in knots at the moment, Auwei said.

True. Right now, I didn't really know what I wanted. My mind couldn't help but compare Prince Alvere with Silence, finding all manner of similarities and differences. They were both short, slight men, not large. The prince had a bit more of a plumpness to his face and features. Alvere had raven black hair and those piercing beryl-blue eyes, compared to Silence's mouse brown hair and soft brown eyes. The real difference was in their demeanor. The prince was strong and commanding. Silence was growing into his power but still mild mannered much of the time. They were both handsome, both good friends.

Well Silence was a good friend. I barely knew the prince.

But you want to know him... intimately, don't you? Auwei offered.

I flushed again at that, as Maverick and I entered the great hall through the outside door. I couldn't quite get the memory of my encounters with Silence out of my mind... and in my musings I kept switching out his face with the prince's.

"Oh... my!" Amber said.

That snapped me out of my reverie.

"You are a rather exquisite shade of crimson, my dear," she said to me. "Who are you thinking of?" And that, of course, only made me blush more.

We called for an early dinner, and I ate with my head down, hoping no one would notice my heated features. And while I ate, I thought of Maverick's words.

... you need to help, to defend, to stand up to those who would push others around...

... You... need to be a hero...

... We know you're going to disrupt the plans of the Nobles behind all of this. You couldn't not do it. It's in your blood. They're bullies, and you'll stop them at any cost...

... you're going to be a handful...

... always... running toward danger, not away...

Was that really true?

I couldn't deny that I'd stood up to a mistweaver, an impossible fight... and won.

Trust in yourself, Legs. Maverick is right. I can feel it. Auwei seemed certain. I wish I could have been.

Then Fin appeared in the great hall with the prince next to him and...

...Silence, laying bloody and limp in Fin's arms.

"He's alive," Fin said reassuringly, though his tone wasn't entirely confident. "Is Ant any better? Silence could use some healing."

Some healing? The man looked dead, covered in cuts and blood and bruises.

The sight was too much. I turned away and threw up everything I'd just eaten.

CHAPTER 3

JACK WAS OFF LIKE A SHOT TO FETCH ANT, EVEN AS AMBER yelled, "He's not ready yet!"

"I'll get bandages," Crane said as she too ran out of the hall.

I looked up, wiping my mouth, as Fin laid Silence on a table.

I stood, but couldn't draw closer. Even from here I could see the horrors done to the man I loved. He'd been tortured. His small, delicate hands were ruined, crushed and swollen. His face was covered in blood, shallow slashes on his lips, ears, nose, and cheeks. Most of his fine clothes had been torn away and what parts of his body I could see were covered in bruises and other injuries. My jaw trembled, clamped shut. I couldn't speak, only rage and weep.

"I'm... so sorry," Alvere breathed.

I couldn't look at him. His people had done this.

"How did they catch him?" Maverick asked, voice hard, stoic. I could hear his repressed rage.

"My people have some secrets—"

"Tell me!" The room suddenly grew deathly cold, frost rimed the insides of the windows.

Spirits Within! Was this Maverick's cold rage? It was terrifying!

Alvere started, and I could see true fear in his eyes. He swallowed hard. "I guess, since we're allies, I can let you know." He drew a heavy, shuddering breath. "My people have had some contact with the Fey, up north of our lands. They have equipped us with some intriguing items. One such is a trap meant for Elistans who can change shape. It attracts all manner of animals to a place and when they get there, forces them into their true shape. Most animals wouldn't be affected but one of your kind..."

Maverick nodded. "Clever." His jaw twitched. I was willing to bet he was as furious as I was, perhaps more.

And yet...

We had been at the palace to spy on the Vauphani. And their king and queen were dead along with a great number of nobles. They too must have been livid and desperate for information. And... finding Silence...

Would I have done this?

Could I do something like this?

If someone came into my house and killed the ones I loved... what would I do?

No, the real question was: What *wouldn't* I do?

Bloody bones, I hated every part of this. Mostly I raged at the corrupt Nobles of my own nation, who'd sent us on this death-mission. But they weren't here.

And Alvere didn't deserve my fury. I knew he hadn't done this to Silence. He'd probably stopped it the moment he'd found out. Still, I couldn't look at him, couldn't bear to see the pain in those clear blue eyes. He wasn't allowed to feel pain too, not now.

"You called?" croaked a weary voice from the doorway. Ant limped into the room, leaning heavily on Jack, who strained under the larger man's bulk.

"You shouldn't be up!" Amber chided. "Even for this." The concern in her voice real, but also torn. She wasn't truly fighting him. She wouldn't stop him from helping Silence, since she could see the massive damage done to the young man. Still, I sensed her concern for Ant. He might cause himself harm. I'd learned that if he went too far to heal another, he could die.

I felt compelled to add, "Please, help him, but... be careful."

Ant smiled at me. "Always."

That was a lie. He hadn't been careful when he'd faced those guards back at the palace, which had landed him in his current state. He'd been fearless, protecting myself and Amber, but not careful.

Jack helped him sit at the table where Silence lay. Ant reached out a trembling hand to the young man. He laid his other thick arm on the table and put his head upon it, clearly weary even before he began.

Amber stood beside him and laid a hand on his back as he worked. I didn't see much of a change in Silence. His hands seemed to mend a little and his face cleared of some of the cuts upon it.

Then two things happened at once. Ant groaned and his hand fell away from Silence, as Silence gasped, then screamed. It was a sound of pure agony, so heart-rending I fell to my knees in sympathetic suffering, covering my ears and weeping. I heard Amber's soft "sleep" command and the screaming stopped. When I looked up again Silence was still.

Crane returned with a heavy bundle of bandages and a

pot of something, which she spread on some of the wounds as she went to work mending the young man.

Amber helped Ant to the floor, for he was close to dead-weight with exhaustion. There he lay and slept.

"Let's give these people some peace," Maverick commanded and the rest of us began to filter out of the great hall. "Silence will live," Maverick said, certainty in his voice. "Let's all give him the time he needs to recover."

I didn't realize I was trembling until Sparrow took my hand. "Let's get you to your room," she said softly and led me, like a witless child, to my bed. There she laid me under the covers, still fully dressed save for my boots, and tucked me in gently. But perhaps seeing my addled state she then curled up with me, one arm around me, hugging me close. Only then, did I begin to come down from the horrors I'd seen.

I woke with a scream. My dreams had been filled with blood and ruined bodies.

The purring form of Princess-as-a-cat lay next to me, not Sparrow. A moment later the pleasantly plump woman sat on the edge of my bed. "I'll tell Sparrow you're awake. We'll make you some tea, yes?"

I nodded, wordlessly, thankful.

Princess smiled and was off, back in cat form, running from the room.

I sat up in bed, bleary-eyed and feeling like I'd spent the previous night drinking heavily. Pulling my knees up, I hugged them and set my weary forehead upon them.

That's how Sparrow found me.

I turned my head, still laying upon my knees, to look at her as she put two steaming cups of tea on the bedstand and sat on the bed, one arm moving to stroke my back.

She spoke in a soft, reassuring voice. "Remember when

you were hurt? Ant stayed by you, sleeping on the floor, resting until he could heal you again. He's doing that for Silence now. They're resting together, and Ant heals Silence when he can. With Ant being so injured and exhausted already, it's slow going, but Silence will recover fully in time. Fear not."

I lifted my head and nodded. "Thank you," I croaked, my voice raw, throat dry.

Sparrow winced, then rose and retrieved the jug of water from my sitting area, along with a cup. She returned and poured some out for me.

I drank as she placed the jug aside.

"Thank you again." I put the cup down on the bedstand next to my tea. Then I reached for Sparrow and embraced her. We held each other tightly for some time.

I was a little surprised when our lips met. Sparrow's were soft and warm as they pressed firmly to mine. But then she drew back quickly, a look of shock in her eyes. She looked down, head tilted away. "Sorry, I..."

I didn't know what to make of all this. What I did know... was how my heart had quickened, how my body had flushed with heat. Curious.

I put a finger under Sparrow's chin and lifted her face.

"It's well," I whispered. Her gaze met mine, and I could see shame mixed with desire in those shimmering dark-green depths. I brushed some of her wayward chestnut-brown hair aside and cupped her cheek, bringing her face back to mine.

I didn't know what I wanted in that moment except another kiss. She was first surprised, then quickly hungry, her lips hard on mine, opening as mine did, our tongues mingling. I felt the full body shudder which shivered through her as she tried to press closer. I didn't dissuade her.

A part of me wanted this, needed this. I was exhausted with worry and horror for Silence and still couldn't dare to think of the prince. But I desperately needed someone, someone to hold tight and press close. I was confused and curious and thrilled all at once. Sparrow was a dear friend. Though it was quickly becoming clear that Sparrow wished for more. Silence had been a dear friend before we had...

Sparrow pulled away suddenly and rose, agitated. A heady blush colored her tanned cheeks.

"I'm sorry, Legs. Now isn't the time... I..." She turned away.

"Sparrow, no, please," I reached out to her as she turned back. "Stay with me."

She blinked.

"Are you sure?" she asked. Her hand clasped mine, so small, but so very warm.

In response I gently pulled her back to sit next to me. "Yes, I need someone to hold right now." I wrapped my arms around her again. Slowly her arms enfolded me as well.

"I'm sorry for the kiss," she breathed, trembling in my arms. "I shouldn't have—"

"Hush," I whispered. "I... liked it."

"You did?" She seemed shocked.

"I did." It was the truth. Kissing her was different, but no less enjoyable than Silence. There was something about the soft, pliable plumpness of her lips...

"I... I think..." I heard her swallow hard. "I think I love you, Legs." Her voice was so soft and tentative, yet her tone held a note of certainty. That hadn't been an idle admission. She didn't mean she loved me as a friend. *That* was a given. She was telling me she wanted more.

I didn't know what to say.

After a moment Sparrow pulled back. "Was that... too

much?" Her eyes welled with tears, even as a fragile and uncertain hope blossomed in those deep green pools. "I... know it's not the time, but... I... I had to say something."

The longing in her gaze told me everything I needed to know, exactly how far beyond friendship her love extended. She wanted more than just to hold me.

And what did I want?

I couldn't say for certain how I felt for her, but I desperately needed the intimacy she was offering. My heart ached for a deep connection, a soothing of pain in mutual comfort.

I didn't know what to say, so instead of words, I leaned forward to give her a soft, chaste kiss. She tensed, surprised.

When I pulled back, I smiled. The words came easily now. "I love you too, Sparrow," I said tenderly. "You are my dearest friend—" I saw her fragile hope dwindle, "—and I *do* want this. I want *you*."

Her breath caught, those already large eyes going wide as her lips trembled.

"Oh Legs, I... how much... do you want?" She was holding back, seeking permission. It was clear she wanted to give me everything, all of herself.

"I want you, Sparrow," I repeated. "All of you." And I kissed her again, with passion, holding nothing back, to show her how much I meant it.

We drank deeply of each other, our hands exploring hidden places until Sparrow was practically vibrating with desire.

She pulled away and slipped off the bed, quickly lifting off her dress. She wore a silken shift beneath and that too was quickly removed. It was perfectly normal to see her like this. It wasn't uncommon for us to bathe together. Yet this time, her body wasn't flushed red from the heat of warm water, but from desire... for me. Her small breasts heaved with heavy breaths, nipples tight with arousal.

She climbed back onto the bed as I threw back the sheets. Her hands trembled with anticipation as she helped me out of my dress. We knelt on the bed, poised but hesitant. Sparrow's gaze devoured me, her breath coming quicker.

Did she want me to make the first move?

No.

She reached out, tentative, her warm hand coming to my hip. From there, she caressed up along my ribs to the side of my chest. I lifted my arms out of her way, combing my hands into my hair. She bit her lip as her hand came to cup my right breast, heavier and fuller than hers. A trembling finger moved to the areola, tracing carefully around the nipple, watching as it rose and tightened before her eyes.

Her gaze rose to mine. "I never thought... I never dared to hope..."

I nodded. Same-sex pairings were common enough in Elista, but I understood how difficult it might be to ask another if they were interested.

She leaned in and kissed me again as her hand continued wonderfully working over my breast. Her other hand rose to do the same on the other side.

Curious myself, I lifted a single hand up between her arms to her chest. I felt the low swells of her breasts, the raised pucker of her areola, and the tight bud of her nipple. Her left breast was slightly larger than the right, but I caressed them both, wishing to return the sensations she was arousing within me.

One of her hands left my breast, moving slowly over my stomach, then between my thighs. She was insistent and firm, her fingers pressing and probing my folds with expert precision. And just like that, this experiment got far more interesting. Unlike a man, Sparrow knew exactly what pleased a woman and ensured I found such pleasure.

Her lips pressed firmer, her kisses growing deep and desperate as her fingers worked in my slick folds, furious and sure. Harder... seeking... Spirits Yes!

I tensed and shook with a sudden release, gasping into her mouth.

She eased off, caressing softly as we collapsed onto my bed, pressed close. It was my turn to slide a hand down between her thighs. Her folds were already wet as I traced the sensitive area. I too knew how to press and rub for maximum effect. I hadn't pleasured myself often, but I'd done enough to know what felt good.

She gasped, then bit her lip. "Oh Legs... I... you..."

I stopped her awkward words with a kiss as I quickened and intensified my massage upon her clit. I felt her legs open, one slim thigh slipping between mine as I leaned closer over her. I moved my lips to the gentle rise of one breast and sucked her hard nipple into my mouth, remembering how exquisite it felt when Silence had done it for me.

Her back arched, rising from the soft mattress as she moaned; needful and profound. She clamped her hand over mine, pressing me hard to her folds as she shuddered with her release.

Her brilliant green eyes flared wide with arousal, pupils dilated, as she gasped through her orgasm. Pulling my face up to hers, she devoured my lips as she took a long moment to finish her blissful convulsions.

I thought us done, but Sparrow took control and rolled me onto my back. I yelped with surprise at the playful turn as she kissed her way down my body, moving between my legs.

She was not as confident or proficient with her lips and tongue as she'd been with her hands, but that didn't make the sensations any less thrilling. Especially once she began using her fingers as well. Two slender fingers slid inside me as her lips sucked on my clit, tongue teasing. The combined pressure from within and without was too much, and I let out an involuntary series of moans as I clenched around her fingers.

She didn't stop, didn't let up, and I found my pleasure only mounting. My hands combed through her hair, gripping and pressing her closer as my hips rocked and rose. Tears of bliss escaped my clamped-shut eyes, tracing over my cheeks. I gasped and shuddered out heaving breaths, whispering "yes" over and over. Until finally she stopped with her lips on my folds and moved up again, her mouth finding my ever-so-sensitive-breasts. And feeling the gentle rake of her teeth on my nipples, as her fingers raged between my legs, I cried out with a final release so powerful it felt like my whole body rose from the bed.

Breathless and trembling with bliss, I could do nothing but ride out this pleasure as Sparrow settled beside me. Her lips teased up my neck to nibble on an ear as she breathed, "Thank you, Legs. I'd always wondered... Now I know."

And now I knew.

Have you ever been with a woman? I asked Auwei. *As a woman?*

This was a first for me too, she said, trembling with her own passion. *Thank Sparrow for me. This I shall not soon forget.*

"Auwei... wants me to... thank you," I gasped through heavy breaths.

"And you?" Sparrow asked tentatively.

"I thank you too," I said, turning to her, kissing those soft lips once again. I felt compelled to do more, however. She'd brought me to the heights of bliss, and I sensed that had been truly joyous for her, but she deserved more. I wasn't sure I'd be as certain in my work but I began to kiss my way down her body.

Sparrow stopped me. A hand on my chin moved my head up to look at her. "Legs, no. you don't have to. I am sated."

"And if I want to?"

I saw her lips press tight. A tear fell from one eye as her breathing grew heavy. She swallowed hard. "Do you? Truly?"

Did I?

In truth I wasn't certain whether I wished to kiss her as intimately as she'd done with me. But I wanted to do more. "I will do what I feel," I said, not really knowing what that meant.

Yet she nodded and let me go. I saw her eyes squeeze shut as she pushed her head back into the pillows, her hands moving to her breasts, stroking the taught nipples and raised areolae.

I kissed over her stomach, seeing it flex and tense, then down to her hips. There I stopped for the awkward moment of moving between her legs. She opened her thighs, pressing them to the sides as I slid my hands under her taut buttocks to lift her.

I was curious...

I pressed my lips to her folds as if they were her lips, in a long and lingering kiss, my tongue exploring her, before lifting away. Her body tensed and trembled before me and I returned to run my tongue over the taut nub of her clit. She gasped and shuddered.

I moved my lips to the inside of her thigh as I slid a

finger within her. Her hips rocked forward and she gasped. The wet warmth of her canal gripped my finger as I stroked her ever-so-sensitive walls.

I kissed my way up her body as I slid a second finger into her folds, my thumb teasing her clit. Her thighs pressed tight around my hand, hips moving against me, her body trembling. When my lips touched hers, both her hands came up to my head, curling in my hair, drawing me breathlessly close. She was desperate and hungry, devouring me.

I found a rhythm, rocking my hand into her, finding the spots which most pleased her and stroking them with fervor. I felt her pleasure mount, body writhing, hips grinding against my hand. She went so tense and tight, like a stretched cord...

Then snapped.

Her body shuddered as a great moan welled up from within her. She tilted her head back, pressed into the bed as open-mouthed, wide-eyed bliss surged through her. I felt her pulsing around my fingers as she gasped and cried out. Her back arched, breasts thrust up at me. I kissed those soft swells as she rode the wave of this orgasm to its end.

After that, we lay in each other's arms for a long time.

Eventually, staring up at the canopy of my bed, Sparrow shook her head slowly. "I can't believe..." She let out a shuddering, "Ohhhhh." Then she rolled her head to look at me, our noses brushing. "You're amazing," she whispered, then bit her lip, those deep green eyes searching mine. "I meant to comfort *you*—"

"And you did, thank you, Sparrow."

"Legs, please, let me finish. I..." She stammered for a moment lost for words. Then she swallowed, pursed her lips, and continued.

"What you've done for me... I... I don't know if this was

just one moment of comfort for you. If so, then I will be forever grateful." She smiled, a shy thing. "Amber had offered, but... I'd never been certain this was what I wanted, to be with... another woman. I always felt it was, but I was never sure. And Amber always seemed... too much, if that makes sense?"

It did.

"But with you, I felt... safe. Now I know: this is what I want. And for that I thank you, from the deepest places in my heart." She kissed me lightly, then licked her lips. "You've given me a precious gift, and if this one time is all you wanted, I'll... I'll understand. I'm glad I could bring you some comfort when you needed it."

I placed a hand on her cheek as I smiled. "And I thank you, Sparrow. I... I will admit, I was uncertain of this, but... now..."

How *did* I feel?

Wonderful. I felt wonderful. This new and amazing experience had been so soft and caring, yet incredibly intense. I wanted more.

Did that change my desire for men? No... it didn't. Apparently, I wanted both men and women. I felt my heart open. This was the *more* I'd been looking for... at least in part. "I want more with you. I love you dearly, Sparrow."

She blushed, a deep and beautiful rose hue upon her soft brown cheeks.

And oddly, this hadn't felt like a betrayal of my love for Silence. I'm not sure I could say why, but I just knew in my soul that he'd understand this *experiment* to explore deeper intimacy with a dear friend. It was exactly what he and I had done. Yet, to go further without him knowing, that felt wrong. I knew now... I wanted more than just one intimate relationship, but everyone involved would need to accept this... amalgamated arrangement.

Exactly, Auwei said. *Though I have never been a part of one, group relationships are accepted in Elista. And from what I hear, as long as everyone knows what's going on and agrees to it, such groups can be quite fulfilling.*

That reminded me of something Ant had said about Jack. He'd warned Silence, saying Jack *goes for all sorts*. Which brought to mind the image of Jack and Silence and Ant all naked and kissing and...

"What are you thinking about?" Sparrow said, voice a little odd. "You're turning beet red."

I felt the heat upon my cheeks and probably wore some bemused look on my face. I shook that off. "Nothing, just... thinking that you've opened my horizons. I think I'd like to be with men *and* women."

"Together?" she asked, eyes wide.

Well... now that you mention it...

Naughty girl.

Yup, that's me.

"Maybe...?"

"Oh." Those beautiful green eyes grew larger still. "I suppose... I could *try* that?" Sparrow said tentatively.

"I won't force you to do anything. But I'll keep that in mind," I said with a mischievous grin.

After that, we lay dozing together for the rest of the morning before our stomachs started to rumble.

We dressed and headed down for — what would now be — lunch.

Once again, Amber was outside my room as the two of us came out. She smiled knowingly at us, then winked and nodded.

Putting an arm around both of us, as we moved down

the hall, she whispered, "Now that you've figured yourselves out, you should come see *me* sometime."

I was curious... so I asked, "what about you and Ant?"

She nodded. "I care for him deeply," she said, but then her voice grew husky. "I care for all of you... deeply."

"Oh."

"Exactly."

I was learning more and more about my housemates.

CHAPTER 4

THE NEXT FEW DAYS PASSED WITH A HUSH OVER THE MANOR AS we all waited and prayed for Silence and Ant to recover.

The prince came and went with Fin, but while he was with us, he was quiet and reserved. I could guess why. He may not have been a part of what had been done to Silence, but since it had been people under his command, he felt responsible. So he remained distant: solemn and quiet. We all avoided him. That was until the third day, when Amber grabbed his arm as he rose after breakfast in the great hall.

"Come with me, princey," she said pulling him to his feet.

He blinked, surprised. "I... ah... I'm not... please, what...?"

She turned her disarming smile on him as we all watched. "You're coming with me and we're going to work out some of your pent-up frustration."

His eyes grew wide, as did most of the rest of ours.

She grimaced. "No, not like that. I'm going to teach you some combat techniques."

"Combat...?" He was clearly confused. "I have been trained..."

"Not like this," she said low and secretive. "You've got a small frame, you're lithe and quick. I think you'll do well with my style."

Ah, so that's what she had in mind. Curious, I rose and followed as she dragged him out of the hall.

"Don't hurt him too much!" Maverick called after them. "He's royalty!"

Sparrow and Foggy trailed along with me as we went to the training room. But it was only once we got there that he turned and saw us. "We're to have an audience?"

Amber, ever on her toes, blinked. "Audience? No, they're here to help you train." She looked at me and tilted her head indicating I should step out. "Go ahead, see if you can get Legs on her back."

I blushed furiously.

"Ah... s-sorry, w-what?" Alvere stammered, also blushing. At least I wasn't the only one. "I'm not dressed for training," he said by way of excuse.

Neither was I, wearing a long, simple dress.

Amber wouldn't let him off that easily, though. "Neither is she. We'll sort out proper dress next time. If you're really worried about it, you could both just take off your clothes."

We both stared at her flatly.

Amber shrugged. "Or not. The point here is to see how good you are at hand-fighting. It doesn't require armor or special equipment, and frankly if this comes up in real life, you're likely to be wearing what you're wearing now. So just humor me. See if you can get Legs on her back on the mats."

The prince looked at me with an apologetic look and shrugged. "I'm sorry," he said as he stepped toward me. Only... it wasn't going to be him who was sorry.

He tried to be gentle, moving close then simply pushing me. It was almost comical how quickly and easily I bested him. His hands came for my shoulders, I reached across, grabbed the one while turning away from the other. Then I pushed his hand back, locking his wrist. I followed that up with my other arm locking the elbow of that same arm and forcing it up... which forced him down, and a moment later I was kneeling next to him, where he lay on his back. I released his arm and wrist, and he pulled them back quickly, massaging them.

"What was that?" he asked, confused and shocked.

"That," Amber said coming to stand over us both. "Was a very basic move. Would you like to learn it?"

The prince nodded. Then he looked at me as we both got up. "I should have known not to underestimate you." He shook his head, still staring at me, and I believe I blushed a little at his scrutiny. "A few days ago, you were cut up beyond reason, and now you're healed and hale as an ox, and it wasn't your healer who did it, was it?"

I shrugged, trying to be mysterious. "I'm just amazing," I said.

"You are." His voice was low and breathy, only for me. I *know* I blushed then.

For the rest of the morning Alvere practiced. It quickly became apparent that though he didn't know this style, he was well trained. He equated certain moves with others he knew from sword-practice or work with staves and pole-arms. That, and he was a quick learner. By the end of the first lesson, he'd learned the lock I'd used on him, plus a few other moves, and before we left for lunch, it was me who was on my back, with him holding my arm at a strange angle.

Sorry, he mouthed the word as he released me. His

sweat-damp hair and flushed cheeks — from the morning's exertions — added to those stunning beryl-blue eyes, were making me sweat for a very different reason. Good thing I was already sweaty and messy and a little bit more wouldn't be noticed.

As he helped me up, I caught sight of Sparrow across the room. Her look toward the prince, along with a slight shrug and tilt of her head gave me all the information I needed: she might be ok with him joining us. I rolled my eyes in return, hopefully telling her we weren't going to be doing anything anytime soon. She smiled and nodded. The prince only caught the end of that.

"You have many close friends here, don't you?" He looked from Sparrow to me. "We don't really know a lot of how your Noble Houses work, given that you select Nobles instead of them being born to their title. Are you all close?"

Some of us were *very* close.

"Yes," I said with a smile. Then, to get the conversation away from that, I said, "I never understood your way. What if a noble isn't meant for rulership? He still gets his title and land when his father dies. And why does it always go through the male, not the female. Our way seems much more logical, based on skill and—"

He laughed. "I suppose so. But your way might have its flaws as well. Only people who *want* to rule are tested. Not all those who want to rule are good rulers. What if there were others who would be good rulers who don't decide to be tested, or aren't even Chosen by Lumani to begin with? What then? And Nobles choosing other Nobles also leads to the possibility of nepotism and favorites, or bribes. I'm not saying being born to it is better, but I don't think either option is perfect."

He had a point. And we'd gotten the conversation away from my personal life. I chatted with him about politics as we made our way back to the great hall for lunch. And we talked all through lunch. We probably would have kept going, if Maverick hadn't interrupted us.

"You two probably don't want to see this, but I think you should both come with me," he said heavily. From his expression, whatever *this* was, wasn't going to be fun. We looked at each other, then back to him.

"What is it?" I asked.

"We're going to question the fake mistweaver."

Oh...

"Fake mistweaver?" Alvere said with a note of horror.

Maverick nodded, then drew a long breath. "The one who... did what she did at your palace, also wanted our dear Legs dead as well. We thought we'd captured her, after she'd attacked us here at Hedgewild, but it was a decoy to make us think we were safe." His expression grew grim. "It's only a theory, but I think she wanted us to let Legs go on that mission, so that she could kill her along with... the others... and make it look like they'd all done it to each other. A convenient scapegoat."

The prince nodded, but there was a shadow over his features. "I thought your mission was to *stop* the mistweaver? But if you thought you had her here, why did you come to my palace?"

Maverick looked at me. "You told him we were sent to stop her?" Maverick nodded to himself. "Ah..." Then he turned and walked away. "This way," he called back to us without otherwise explaining anything. He was going to leave the truth to me.

Great.

I hoped the prince wouldn't ask, but as we rose to follow Maverick, Alvere looked at me. "What are you not telling me?"

I sighed. No use in denying it now. "Once we *knew* the mistweaver was there, it *became* our mission to stop her," I said.

That's still not the truth, Auwei said, and I got the impression of her shaking her head, even though she'd never had a head.

I know! But... it's close enough.

If you insist.

I do.

Still, I owed the prince more of an explanation, so I went on. "Our original mission was to find out if you were planning war against us."

His brow furrowed further. "So... wait... you were sent to find out if we were planning war? But you'd already invaded our lands."

"Not me, not us here. We didn't know anything about the war."

"But other Elistans..." He shook his head. "You really didn't know... and even the person who ordered you to go didn't know."

"Or they did know," I said with a grimace as Maverick led us down a set of stairs into the basement of the west wing. "And they were setting us up to fail and be scapegoats."

"That's horrible. Your own people...?"

"Yeah, exactly. That's why we trust you more than our own right now."

He nodded. "I see."

I was glad he'd taken the truth well. He could have been

very upset with us, with me, but he actually seemed sympathetic. That was a load off my mind.

We reached the bottom of the stairs. The basement was quite dark. Early on in my time at Hedgewild, I had done a perfunctory exploration of the basements, but hadn't stayed long. There was no natural light and the narrow corridors, with cold stone walls, weren't the friendliest of places.

Maverick snapped his fingers and several torches lit themselves along the dark stretch.

The prince and I paused, looking down the eerily quiet hallway as torch light cast dancing shadows upon the gloomy walls.

Maverick led on and we followed, hushed to silence now. When we got to a heavy iron door, Maverick got out keys, but then tested the door, it was unlocked. I was curious about this until we entered and saw Amber and Jack within. They had a single lantern shedding light on the long room with barred cells along the far wall. With another snap of his fingers the lanterns were lit and the room grew brighter. I could clearly see the dungeons of Hedgewild now.

They weren't dank and gross, like I'd assumed. The cells looked to be roughly ten feet by ten feet with stone walls on three sides and a wall of iron bars along the front. All the cells contained a cot for a bed and a built-in basin, which I guessed could be filled with water for washing, as well as a not-so-private privy in the far corner. Two of the cells looked used, though only one was occupied. By "used" there were rushes on the floor and the bed was made up and water in the basin.

"We just moved her over," Jack said to Maverick. I didn't quite understand this, but I did then notice that there was a small metal door in the stone wall between every other cell, specifically there was one between the occupied cell and the other "used" cell.

Amber — intuitive as usual — slipped back to whisper to the prince and me. "We move any prisoners from one cell to another every other day to safely clean the now empty cell."

That made sense.

Maverick approached the bars, and I stepped forward to focus on what was to come. The woman inside looked... normal, a bit small of stature and plain of features with light brown hair and brown eyes. She sat neatly on the side of her bed in a long plain dress.

"You've finally come to question me?" she asked Maverick. "It will do you no good. I know nothing."

"We'll see about that," Maverick said, cold and hard. "You were gifted great powers. That is indisputable. Who gave you those powers?"

"The mistweaver," the woman said evenly. "I don't even know her name. She offered me enough gold to live happily for the rest of my life if I did as she asked."

"And what did she ask?"

"She said she would gift me with great power for a limited time. And during that time, my mission was simple: find and kill her." The woman pointed at me.

The cold way she said it sent a chill down my spine.

"Why?" Maverick's tone was as hard as the stone walls around us.

"I didn't ask. I did it for the gold, remember."

Maverick gave an odd sounding grunt-growl but nodded. "How did she indicate the person to be killed?"

I was curious about that as well. Had someone painted a portrait of me? I didn't recall sitting for one.

"She made an image in the mists. Looked exactly like that girl there. That's how I knew."

That made me shiver. It seemed the mistweaver could do almost anything. No one knew the extent of a mistweaver's powers, and that mystery sent a chill down my spine. At the same time, I felt just a little more bad-ass that I'd killed her.

"Who were you before?" Maverick asked.

The woman's demeanor shifted, becoming hard, shoulders set, jaw tight. It took her a moment to answer. "When I was six my parents sold me to a whorehouse. I cleaned and kept house for them until I was old enough to join those illustrious ranks. But I was not gifted with beauty, as you might see, and did not bring in much coin for my mistress. And, since she'd acquired a new cleaning girl by then, I was kicked out onto the streets to beg. I did what I had to, in order to survive, until that madwoman came along. Her offer was easy to accept. Kill one person for a wealth of coin?" The woman shrugged. "I'd not tried killing yet, but I'd been close. And to get away from that life, it seemed a fitting task."

"That's horrible," Alvere whispered to me.

I had to agree. Though I still didn't have a lot of pity for this woman who'd tried to kill me.

"Did you hear the mistweaver say anything about why she wanted this woman dead or who else might be involved?"

The woman smiled wide, with mock-innocence. "I didn't ask, and she didn't offer. I was a bit confused why a mistweaver would need the help of a wretch like me, but I see that clearly now. I was never meant to succeed. Only wear her face and be a decoy. Am I right?"

Maverick grunted a non-comital sound.

The woman nodded. "As I thought. What will you do with me?"

Maverick's tone was hard. "You will remain here and be well cared for until such time as you are needed to testify to what you have done before the Council of Nobles."

The woman shrugged at that. "At least it's mostly warm and mostly dry. More than I can say for my life beforehand." She lay back on the bed, though she left one leg over the side and as she put the other one on the bed, her dress rode up high on her legs. "And I'll be here if any of you men need my services."

Maverick turned away sharply and returned to us. "There is nothing here. I'm sorry."

"That's the reaction I usually got," the woman said with a sigh.

"No one is to touch her, is that understood?" Maverick said sternly.

Not that it needed saying, even Jack was shaking his head. "That goes without saying, Boss."

We left the dungeons, locking the door behind us, and Maverick bristled, seemingly shaking off the disgust of that experience. Then he sighed heavily. "I'd been putting that off and now I know why. I didn't suspect she knew much, and I knew I wouldn't like the experience."

"It had to be done," Amber said softly.

"What if she was lying?" the prince asked. "What if she made that all up?"

"She didn't," Amber said. "Before you arrived I... made her speak the truth."

"You can do that?"

Amber looked into his eyes for a long moment and stepped in close, whispering to him: "Tell me you love me."

"I love you," he said without hesitation.

"Forget that," she said. And he blinked and shook his head.

"What...?"

I took his hand. "I'll explain later," I said with a sour look at Amber. She shrugged. Maverick growled at her. That made her laugh.

We were an odd crew.

CHAPTER 5

Days turned to weeks. With Ant not at full strength, it took some time for him and Silence to heal.

I distracted myself, spending my time with Sparrow, or in training. I also talked with Prince Alvere, whenever he was with us. I loved to learn of his kingdom and he listened intently as I spoke of my home. We were becoming... friends. A part of me wanted more, he was handsome and intelligent and seemed interested in me.

But I'd do nothing more than get to know the man before talking to Silence. He was my first partner and I'd not explore my desires to expand my sphere of relationships without his consent. Yet Silence slept most of the time, still recovering.

So I had to wait.

I spoke to Sparrow about the prince. She thought him handsome as well, but wouldn't say much more than that. She wanted me to be happy, but she also knew how I felt for Silence.

The trouble was... some of my combat training with Alvere got quite intense. He was a good student and quickly became a match for me. If I didn't use my avatar abilities, he'd win as often as lose. And we were both competitive, so we got a little... overzealous at times. Amber would watch us as we sparred, shaking her head, eyes wide.

I gulped in air, breathing hard, backed against the wall during one of our fights. He too huffed heavy breaths, sweat on his brow and soaking through his practice shirt. Something about him seemed harder now. I think he'd lost the last of the boyish roundness in his features. Perhaps we'd been training him too hard.

He swept a kick to knock me off my feet, but I jumped. And for just an instant I used my abilities to plant my feet against the wall behind me and launch myself at him bodily. I hit him hard and we both tumbled to the mats, rolling over each other. He ended up on top and quickly pinned my right arm. I punched with my left, not as strong, but still hoping to stun him with a hit to the kidneys. But I only brushed his shirt as his hand clasped over my wrist stopping my strike. He smiled down at me.

"Now what?" he asked with a note of victory.

"Now you learn how to truly fight one of us," I said with a grin. Planting my feet, I used all my strength to buck him off me, though I may have been a little too zealous. He released me as he flew over my head, flipping forward.

I spun and rose to a ready-kneel, facing where he would land.

To his credit, he managed to land on his feet and did an awkward, off-balance spin back to face me. I swept his legs. He tried to jump, but I caught enough of his right foot to cause him to fall to his left. Then I was on him, straddling him, like he'd done with me a moment before. I pinned his left arm, his dominant hand.

I was unable to catch his right-handed strike and he hit

me hard, just under the ribs. I grunted, but didn't release his arm. Still, that had hurt — I'd have a nasty bruise tomorrow — and I didn't want to leave myself open for another punch. So... I dropped low over him, pressing myself to him, faces inches apart, then I softly dipped in to kiss his cheek. I needed to end this fight and knew one way to do that.

"Surrender or you get the lips," I whispered.

He raised a single brow. "That's cheating," he huffed, breathless.

"Yeah, but I like fighting dirty."

He shook his head and tapped out with his free hand.

"Good boy," I said, kissing him again on the cheek. That second kiss hadn't been needed, but looking into those perfect blue eyes always got my blood pumping and I'd acted without thinking. That made me wonder if I'd have had poison on my lips if I *had* kissed him. I certainly wasn't feeling fear or animosity right now. No, mostly I wanted to keep pressing myself against him and kiss those beautiful full lips, while he kissed me back.

But... I couldn't, not yet.

I got one leg under me and did a back flip off him.

"Show off," he said, then did a flawless kip-up.

"Who's showing off now?"

He grinned and shrugged.

"Well," Amber said approaching us. "You know enough of the basics that you should have a much easier time defending yourself against attackers while unarmed." She looked back and forth between the two of us. To the prince, she said: "I think you'll be headed back to your own lands soon. I hear the war in the North is escalating."

He nodded slowly. "I'll be back here as often as I can, but I need to be there for my troops."

"Oh?" I said, surprised at the distress in my voice. "Leaving so soon?"

He smiled. "Not quite yet, but soon. And from what I hear, so too will you."

I was a bit surprised at that. I looked at Amber, who nodded. Though she then gave the prince a scathing look. "That was not to be mentioned yet."

He shrugged. "She should know sooner rather than later."

Amber grimaced. "Fine." She turned to me. "Once Silence is well, which seems like it will be soon. A group of us will be heading to the capital."

Oh... From how Alvere had phrased it, I thought I might have been going with him. Now... I was conflicted. I wanted to be with him *and* Silence...

"Even me?" I said, a bit surprised. "Aren't there people in the capital who want to kill me? I thought I was to lay low?"

Amber's grimace quirked into a half-smile. "Boss seems to think we won't be able to stop you from going with us. He thinks you can handle it. Also, we've got a plan for you."

"A plan?" Why did I keep saying these inane two-word sentences?

"Yeah, you'll be going on the pretense of visiting your sister. She and her House should provide some protection for you. Also..." and with this she glanced at the prince with a slightly sour note. "Midnight will be keeping an eye on you."

"They didn't want to tell me about their secret weapon," the prince said with a laugh. "But I insisted there be no secrets. Though, to be fair, I don't know anything about this Midnight other than her name."

"In truth, I don't know much more than that," I said with a shrug.

I was a little overwhelmed. I'd be leaving soon? Going to see my sister? That would be fun... maybe... if I wasn't worried for my life the entire time. And seeing Midnight for the first time would be interesting. But oddly, it wasn't any of that which was foremost on my mind. No, I was mostly sorry the prince would be leaving, or more precisely that I'd be away from him.

Spirits woman, make up your mind! I shouted at myself.

Auwei laughed. *You're young and free. I've had hosts who were far more promiscuous than you. At least you've only been with those with whom you are truly close. I had one host who would sleep with any man who was remotely handsome. That was an... interesting lifetime, that one. I learned a lot.*

You'll have to share that with me sometime.

Maybe. Or maybe I'll let you learn it for yourself. It can be quite enjoyable to go through that particular learning process.

I bet.

The prince escorted me back to my room after practice. It was late afternoon and we'd need to be ready for supper soon, but we had a little time and I intended to have a bath.

"Legs?" Alvere said tentatively.

I looked over at him. The usually confident young man was hedging, lips pursed, looking at the floor. When he did look back at me, those bright blue eyes catching mine, something seemed to unlock within him. "I will dearly miss you, while I'm away, while we're both away."

"I will miss you too," I said and meant it.

"Might I have a kiss to remember you by?" he asked.

My heart was racing, now that those words had been spoken.

Though then he quirked his mouth. "A kiss that won't make me stiff all over that is."

No, just stiff in one place, Auwei said with a giggle.

Auwei, shame on you!

You were thinking it too.

Maybe.

"I think I could arrange that," I breathed, feeling heat rise within me, blood pumping, my entire body responding to this simple request.

He leaned over a bit, but I raised a hand. "Not now, please. We're both a little... ripe. I'd like to clean up first."

He smiled. "Yes, you're right, of course."

"After dinner, meet me in the reading alcove at the far back of the third level of the library," I said, laying a hand on his chest. I could feel his heart pounding.

He nodded. "I'll see you there."

And that was it. We had a date.

I slipped into my room and leaned with my back against the door for a long moment, waiting for my heart to settle. When it did, I stripped off my practice clothes and left them in the laundry hamper. Then I slipped on a bathrobe and headed to the first floor and a bath.

The upstairs hall was deserted, but as I came out of the stairwell, I saw the prince, in his own robe, heading for the bathing room. He was well ahead of me and there would be no chance of us running into each other if I stayed back. Also, there were separate bathing rooms for men and women. I reached the short hall, off the main hall, which had a door on either side at the end, leading to the two rooms and...

...the door to the men's baths was just a little open. The latch hadn't fully caught after the prince had gone in.

Auwei laughed. *Naughty girl.*

What? Why?

I know what you're thinking. You want to peek in there, don't you?

And the truth was, I'd been about to do just that, so I couldn't really deny it. *Well, then, I'm glad you're on board, I'll just take a quick look. I probably won't see anything anyway.*

I put my eye to the narrow crack between door and frame... just in time to see the prince's robe fall away.

There were four baths to a room. The stone of the foundation had been carved out to make the sunken baths quite large, easily big enough for two people to lounge comfortably. There was even a seat within the bath, the stone rounded and smooth to make it comfortable on one's skin. There were no showers here at Hedgewild, but the baths were maintained through some strange mechanism such that pulling a cord got hot water added to one of the baths. And once you were done, a separate cord would drain the water away.

At this particular angle, peering through the crack, I was only able to see one of the baths, but that had been the one the prince had chosen. He pulled the cord, then waited. The room grew warm as hot water poured into the bath. The prince leaned against a wall, sighed and... his penis twitched to life, rising slightly.

Oh! I flinched back from the crack and quickly took a look around.

No one there.

I debated leaving then. I should give the man some privacy, but I'd been just a little too curious about him. My heart raced and I was sure he'd be able to hear it from where he was. I'd only wanted to see him unclothed I hadn't meant to see... *that.* Apparently, he was thinking of something arousing. And now... so was I.

I dared to look back and found him stroking himself, eyes still closed, a soft, slow caress of his length. I watched, fascinated. His hand moved over his shaft, twisting and sliding along like he was his own lover, even stopping to squeeze the tip a moment, which caused a shuddering breath from him. Yet he remained hard and kept up his work, protracting his pleasure until finally the bell rang signaling the bath was full. He stepped in then, descending the steps into the hot waters, gasping a little. After that, I could see little but his head above the water. I sighed and turned away.

And there was Amber, leaning against the wall behind me, with a smirk on her face. Her bathrobe wasn't of the heavy, soft material like mine, but sheer and silken. She'd clearly caught me peeking and shook her head before silently going into the lady's bathing room.

I had been warm and flushed before, but got super-heated with embarrassment as I stood there for a moment, then followed her in.

She disrobed as her bath filled.

"Wish to share?" she asked. She wasn't making any comment about my indiscretion.

I didn't want to share, but it would save water. I nodded, though I waited to disrobe until the bath was ready. I slipped in quickly as Amber sat on the cold stone rim and dangled her legs in the hot waters.

"I'm sure he'd welcome you, if you asked him," she said softly. "There are ways to bar these doors. It wouldn't be the first time a man and woman have shared a bath before."

Yup, there it was. Luckily now, with hot waters upon me, I had a reason to be flushed beet red.

I couldn't rightly deny anything so I just sighed. "I... don't know what I want with him yet. We're going to meet after supper to, ahh, kiss." That sounded so innocent yet so wrong at the same time.

"Just kiss?"

"I don't know yet."

"Do you want more? You may want to figure that out before you go tonight. If you don't want more, tell him first. Otherwise, it can be hard to stop things later, if you become... swayed."

That was good advice. The trouble was, I didn't know what I wanted with Alvere. Or rather, I *did* know, but couldn't allow it. I wanted to fully explore my feelings for the prince, but wouldn't do that until I'd spoken to Silence first.

It occurred to me, Amber might be a font of information on this.

"How does one keep... several lovers?" I asked a bit tentatively.

Carefully, Auwei said within me.

"With a great deal of care," Amber said echoing Auwei's thoughts. "It is often good to let all parties know that they are not the only ones. Otherwise, it can lead to confusion, anger, and heartbreak. Get that out in the open first, let them know you do not plan to be with just them. See if that's something they're willing to abide by. Some men and women will have no problem with that. Others will want you all to themselves. It's just who they are."

Exactly.

Sorry, I know I'd already talked to you about this, but...

No problem. Amber's information will be more... up to date. My particularly promiscuous host lived over a hundred years ago. Times were different then. Not to mention that my host didn't much care about what others thought, she was in it for the challenge of the chase and the thrill of conquest.

Amber smiled at me. "Are you finding the attentions too much?" she asked, with a tilt of her head. Her auburn hair fell to one side. It was an action meant to draw attention to her, and she knew it. She was playing with me now. She knew I'd been with Sparrow. Was this an invitation?

"Ah... no, not yet, just..." How could I say this? Well, I didn't have to mince words with Amber at least, she knew everyone I'd been with. "I love Silence. He's a kind man, caring and wonderful. And... I don't think he'd fault me getting some comfort from Sparrow, that's... different. But... from another man?"

Amber nodded. "Ah, yes I see."

As much as I wanted to explore a relationship with Alvere, I couldn't... yet. That much I knew. The question was: would a kiss, or a bit of play, still be betraying Silence? I also had to consider that it wouldn't just be the actions themselves, but who I was doing them with. Silence had been tortured by the Vauphani. Though it hadn't been the prince who'd done it, Silence wasn't likely to feel kindly toward anyone from Vauphan.

I sighed heavily.

"You have two options it seems," Amber said as she slid over the edge into the bath with a shuddering sigh of contentment. "Have your fun and check in with Silence later, or wait for Silence and then... have your fun." She shrugged.

The trouble was... "I don't know if the prince will still be around when Silence is done recovering."

Amber nodded. "I see the problem." Then with a silken smile and curious tilt of her head, she asked, "is there anyone else you're interested in?"

"No, of course not!" I said quickly.

Oh? Auwei said innocently. *I'm pretty sure you've had some inappropriate thoughts about Ant, Jack, and Amber herself. Not to mention how much of a hunk Maverick is.*

I... what? No. I... If I hadn't been beet red before, I was now. *You can be quiet now.*

Amber smiled. "I assume your Lumani is well experienced, but just in case Auwei is a prude, if you ever need any... lessons on things. Let me know," Amber purred. She made no move to draw closer to me. It wasn't an invitation, just an offer. She wasn't even looking at me. Her eyes were closed as she leaned her head back against the rim of the bath.

We were both silent after that.

I couldn't figure out what to do. Should I see the prince? Would a single kiss be anything for Silence to worry about? Would it be *a single* kiss? Should I just wait? These questions spun in my mind long after Amber had left the baths. The water was cool by the time I remembered to dunk under and give my hair a scrub. There were soaps around the bath and I quickly washed myself before retreating back to my room.

I'd missed the start of supper. Coming in late, I saw Maverick, Crane, Amber, and the prince huddled together at a far table. I sat alone and ate quietly, all the while anticipating — and now also dreading — my meeting with Alvere that evening.

CHAPTER 6

THESE HIDDEN ALCOVES WERE MY FAVORITE PLACES IN THE library. Small reading nooks, laid with soft cushions, sat beneath tall windows for light. The shelves of books extended out from the walls creating a mostly private area. My heart pounded with excitement and fear as I waited, still unsure of what I wanted.

I should have talked to Silence. He was doing better, with only a few injuries remaining upon him, but he was still fragile and feverish. I didn't want to unsettle his rest with questions like this. But that meant I wasn't sure how I wanted this encounter to go.

A single kiss won't hurt, it's harmless, I told myself.

Then why did you wear your flirtiest outfit? Auwei asked.

That was an excellent question. I'd found this particular outfit before leaving Elista, a matching top and skirt in brilliant rose-gold. The top was actually fairly modest, with a high, round neckline, tight across the shoulders and the tops of the arms, leaving the rest of the arm bare. The slightly scandalous part of the top was that it stopped mid stomach. It was loose and gave some shape to my breasts, but hung off of them, leaving a space between the sheer fabric and my skin.

The skirt was a matching color, sitting a little lower than most, exposing the tops of the hips and all of my lower back, not to mention a good swath below my navel. From there it flared out ending just below the knee. I hadn't had a real reason to wear it in all the time I'd been at Hedgewild. Now I didn't know if I loved it or regretted it.

Alvere peeked around a corner and smiled when he saw me. My earlier assessment of him hadn't been wrong, he'd toned up and lost the roundness on his face. The rest of him — as I'd seen earlier in the baths — had little roundness at all, with fine tight muscles over his slight frame. He was in a deep blue jerkin, white shirt beneath, and cream-colored pants.

He stopped, once he was fully around the corner, and I saw him swallow hard as his eyes grew wide, looking at me. I'm sure I imagined it — my mind still a little stuck on seeing him naked earlier — but I thought I saw a slight bulge in his pants.

Spirits, he looked good.

I was even more confused and torn. My body was clear in its desire for Alvere: racing heart, dry mouth, and a building wet heat between my legs. But my mind still whispered: *what of Silence?*

Alvere approached slowly. "You're... amazing," he whispered. There might be others in the library below. It was one of the reasons I'd suggested here instead of one of our rooms. In a room, we'd be alone, here we were... mostly alone with a constant unknown. "I have seen many beautiful women. As prince there is an endless parade of noble-women who wish to become princess and queen. Some of them were quite attractive, but... you... you outshine them all, Legs." He gave a breathy laugh. "Even your name... I... can't say it without thinking of that part of you." He swallowed hard once again as he stopped, standing over me.

He certainly had lots of flowery words that made me feel seen and loved and pretty.

I stood, heart pounding with a strange mix of uncertainty and desire. He'd been close, and once I was standing, less than a foot of space remained between us. We stood there, in silence, gazing at each other for a long moment. Then one of his hands rose and came to rest on the exposed skin at the top of my hip, then slid up to my waist. Just that soft touch, the brush of movement, sent a thrill through me. I was getting *very* hot and my body trembled with need.

Spirits!

I didn't know whether to flee from him or throw myself into his arms.

I gulped air and saw his eyes dip to watch my heaving chest.

"I... I don't know..." he began, gazing down at his hand and my hip. "Please tell me, Legs, what will happen here? I do not wish to presume. And... I should tell you: I probably can't be with you in a lasting way. I may have to marry one of those other noble-women someday. But until then I can... kiss who I like. And I would very much like to... kiss you. I would like... more too." His gaze rose to mine, beryl-blue eyes bright and intent. "What do *you* want?"

And there it was.

What did I want?

I wanted to move against his hand, feel his touch on my skin, over my hip and across my belly, or around back to pull me close. I wanted his lips on mine, his hands... everywhere, but... even that seemed like too much. Even if it didn't lead to more, I'd essentially be opening the door for

Alvere and I didn't know if I could do that without talking to Silence first.

But all of this had come from him asking for a simple kiss. Perhaps... just that then? Lots of people kissed who weren't lovers.

That's a fine line, Auwei said, cautioning me. *What you say is true, but we both know he wants more, and you want more. So even a chaste kiss might become... more.*

She was right. But I had to tell him something.

"Just a kiss," I breathed the words, voice tremulous and weak. I might as well say what I knew we were both feeling, echoing Auwei's words. "I know I want more, and I know you want more, but we can't have it, not yet. I... I have some things I need to work out first. I hope you understand."

He nodded and gave a faint smile. "Yeah, I understand, my life is complicated too. I already mentioned that who I marry won't be up to me, most likely." He stepped in, close enough to feel the heat of his body, close enough that every one of my heaving breaths brushed my breasts across his tunic. He'd never feel it, but I did. The faint friction aroused my nipples, which stood against the sheer fabric of my blouse.

The pull between us was so strong I could barely breathe. I raised my hand to his shoulder, my touch light since I didn't know if I wanted to push him away or pull him closer.

His voice was just as hot and breathy and needful as mine when he said, "I want... all of you, Legs. But, if all I can have now, is a kiss, I'll take it."

Oh, be so very careful Legs, Auwei warned. *You two are both so hot right now, one kiss might start a fire you can't put out.*

Then I'll trust you to stop it for me... please. I already knew she was right and I didn't trust myself to stop at just a kiss anymore.

Understood, I'll stop you, if you need it.

Oh, I was going to need it. *Thank you,* I said sincerely.

I could trust Auwei to keep me safe from... myself.

Then Alvere tilted his head and I did the same. I don't know whether it was he who moved in or I, but our bodies pressed closer.

And then his lips met mine.

He didn't go stiff this time, well at least not all of him.

The kiss was soft and chaste as we tasted each other, savoring this moment of initial sweet contact. His hand remained on my hip. My hand remained on his shoulder. I thought I could feel his heart thundering in time with mine. Our bodies seemed to vibrate together, with the same intensity.

His hand slipped around behind me, and with the low-slung skirt, he pressed very low on my back, still flesh to flesh.

That simple movement caused a faint moan from me and I opened my lips to his. He responded in kind and our once modest kiss became hungry and deep. We'd moved from appetizers to the main course, and we were famished.

Legs! Auwei shouted at me.

It took all my effort to push away from him and break that contact. My eyes remained closed, lips still moving, remembering his taste and touch.

"Too much?" he breathed.

No.

"Yes," Auwei said through me.

Hey!

I'm only doing what you asked.

I shouldn't have been angry at her. I was angry at myself... but I was petty and redirected that anger at her.

It's your life, Legs. Make this mistake if you like.

But you'll regret it for eternity? It was a favorite saying of hers.

No, Legs. Not this one. This one you'll regret. She sounded sad, disappointed.

Well... Pits!

"I understand," Alvere breathed, but neither of us moved any farther apart. We stayed so very close: lips near but not touching, hot breath mingling. I wanted to taste him again, but I knew if I did... I'd not stop there.

For just a moment, I allowed that fantasy to play out in my mind. The rough, hard kiss as our mouths devoured each other. The needful press of his hands beneath my clothes: the grasp of a breast, the caress of my folds. He'd free his erection, barely even dropping his pants as I wrapped my legs around him, driving him deep within me. He'd take me, standing, pressed back to a bookshelf as we gasped and tried not to make too much noise, just in case anyone else was in the library. It would be so very intense, quick, and needful. We'd both reach a spike of heated passion as we released together, panting into each other's mouths.

The vision was so real to me I had to press my legs together to restrain my arousal.

I gasped and finally pushed away from him, backing off a half step.

"I really hope," I said between heavy breaths, "we can continue this... later." I brought a hand up to cup his cheek. "I *want* you, Alvere," I breathed.

"I want you too," he said, eyes sparkling like gems.

"But now is not the time." I pulled away from him and

drew a long shuddering breath. "I hope we get... a time," I whispered.

"As do I," he breathed. He swallowed hard as his gaze traced over me, as if trying to capture this moment in his mind. "I don't think I'll ever feel for anyone what I feel for you. I don't care if I'm married or not, when you say you are ready, I will always be willing."

Wow... just... wow.

I nodded, not sure I trusted myself to say anything, as I was on the verge of throwing myself at him. Then I carefully moved around him and walked away.

I had to pleasure myself that night. I imagined a slight man with me, inside me, needing me... yet the face on that man kept shifting from Alvere to Silence and in the end, I was left only frustrated.

CHAPTER 7

As you will see, for some of what is to come I was not there to witness it firsthand. I relied on accounts from others. So perhaps I should begin with some of those now...

Silence

Silence woke with a groan, sitting up slowly. It was the first time he'd felt comfortable doing so without help. He looked around and was a bit surprised to find his room empty. Before now, someone had always been there, tending to him. That and Ant had remained close, resting on the floor or a couch, but was gone now.

Strong, slanting beams of sunlight shone through the large windows. That made him smile. A beautiful, sunny day always lifted his spirits. But then, so did simply being in this bed, in this place. His smile widened just thinking about the impossibility of having been chosen for a Noble House. He thought he'd reached the limits of his smiling, but then he recalled who he was here with and his smile grew again.

Legs.

He fell back into his pillows with a sigh. Then felt a thrill at the memory of his encounters with her. He loved everything about her: those large, russet-brown eyes, that soft, wavy hair, her wide cheery grin, the slight up-turn of her nose, and so much more. He couldn't think about the rest without a specific part of him growing stiff and uncomfortable.

His smile faded at the thought that he wouldn't see her for a while. She'd left Hedgewild. Though, in all fairness... he was just happy she was alive.

She'd come to see him yesterday. He'd been a bit feverish, but lucid enough to recognize her and understand that she was truly alive. Before that, others had told him she'd not only survived the mistweaver but defeated her! He hadn't believed them. He'd thought their words the kind lies that you tell someone who's suffering so as not to worsen their condition. But then... there she was, alive and radiant!

She'd been happy to see him doing well and hugged him. That had been the delight of his day. She'd hedged a little and said there was something she needed to talk to him about, but he hadn't paid much attention to that, simply reveling in her aliveness, not to mention her body pressed to his. Later that day, she, Maverick, Amber, and Sparrow had left. They'd been waiting until they knew he would be well. And he was now, though his memory was fuzzy on everything that had happened since the palace. He remembered the terror of the mistweaver, and Legs' bravery, staying behind to aid his escape with information Elista would need. But... after that... things were a blur.

He heard the door to his room open, and someone came

in, whistling. Jack appeared around the corner from the entrance hall, completely naked, of course. Not who Silence wished to see naked at that point, though he couldn't deny that the tall man had an exquisite physique with long, slender muscles. Jack was carrying a tray of food and sauntered in to set it on Silence's bed-side table.

"You're up? And you look well. Good. Have something to eat and we'll talk."

Silence sat up again and carefully lifted the tray over to his lap as Jack sat on the side of the large bed.

"What do you remember?" Jack asked. "From... the palace?"

"Not much, everything's a bit fuzzy." Silence then bit into a thick, warm slice of bread and savored the soft texture.

"Good, very good."

"Amber did that, didn't she?" he said around his mouthful. "There's something you don't want me to remember?"

Jack nodded. "Exactly. And you don't want to remember it either. Trust me. But since you'll probably always be curious, I'll tell you what you need to know. You were caught by the Vauphani and tortured. But their prince, who is our ally now, stopped them and brought you home. You were in a bad way but you're better now, that's all that counts."

Silence nodded. Now he knew the facts without remembering the experience, and could see the benefit in that. Still... a chill ran through him. He recalled the pain and his long recovery well enough, even if he had been delirious. He'd make it a point never to be captured again.

"When do you think you'll be up for a trip?" Jack asked.

"A trip? Where are we going?"

"The capital."

Silence raised a brow. That's where Legs and the others had gone. He'd love to see her again. "Anytime, I'd love to catch up with... the others." He bit into a piece of bacon from the tray, crisp and smokey.

Jack grimaced and shrugged. "We'll see. We might see them, if things work out, but we've got a different mission, you, me, and Foggy. We're going to do some spying."

Silence shuddered, remembering — what he did recall — of the last secretive mission. "What about Vauphan?" he asked. Jack had mentioned something about their prince being an ally, but Silence wasn't sure how that could be possible.

Jack sighed. "Ah...yeah, the situation there has changed a little."

Silence raised his other brow at that. "Oh?"

"We're now friends with Vauphan. After Legs defeated the mistweaver, she subdued their prince and brought him back here."

She'd done that *after* having fought the mistweaver? "All by herself?" Silence asked around some dried fruit and hard cheese.

"No, Amber helped. Anyway, it turns out we had the whole thing backward. Vauphan was planning war, but only as a counter-attack. Apparently, someone in Elista has been taking their northern territories without telling the rest of Elista. We also figured out that our being sent to Vauphan was probably a ruse, to frame us for the death of the king and queen. Oh, and you probably don't know, but the mistweaver we captured here was a fake, probably to get us to drop our guard and send Legs on that mission to Vauphan, so she could be killed."

That was a lot of information to take in, and Silence sat for a long moment simply trying to absorb it.

"So... someone in Elista is behind all of this... even the war?"

Jack nodded. "Exactly. Which is why we're being sent to spy... on our own Nobles."

Silence had been in on Maverick's secret talk a while back, and heard that some Elistan Nobles had killed others, somehow killing their Lumani as well. He knew there was trouble here in Elista, and understood the need to uncover what was going on, but... "You're sure we can trust the Vauphani?" Silence didn't. He may not remember being tortured, but the pain had been real. He didn't much like how things had changed.

Jack shrugged. "Am I sure? No. But the Boss is. Maverick trusts the Vauphani prince, and I trust the Boss. That's good enough for me."

Silence nodded slowly at that. He trusted Maverick too. He'd have to come to terms with this on his own.

"What will you need me to do?" Silence asked.

Jack grinned. "We can get into the details later, but mostly, be your mousy self and get into all sorts of interesting places around the capital, then listen in on things. Foggy will be doing the same. I can't get into the same places you two can, so I'll be running things behind the scenes."

"Understood," Silence said. Then, "I do hope we get a chance to see the others."

"Missing Legs?"

Silence was a bit surprised the other man had gone straight there. He'd thought his relationship with Legs a secret... mostly.

Jack grimaced nodding. "Yeah, no need to say anything I can see it in your eyes." The other man then drew in a long breath and shook his head. "You're going to need to get in line, I think. She's becoming a sought-after woman." He looked off toward one of the windows. "I can't blame you. She's... something else."

Was Jack interested in her as well? And what did he mean by *a sought-after woman*?

But then Jack swung his deep brown-eyed gaze around to Silence and there was a certain appraising look in that glance. "But then... you're not so bad yourself."

Silence was suddenly aware that he was wearing very little, the bed sheets and the tray on his lap covering him to his hips, but nothing above that.

Jack smiled and winked. "My offer still stands. If you ever get tired of chasing that hen and would like to see what a cock is like, let me know."

Silence was flattered. He'd had always found both the male and female forms attractive and Jack was a handsome man. He had no memory of his parents and, for a while, when he'd been living on the streets, he'd stayed with a couple, two men. It was the only time he'd seen an example of true love. Right now though, he was a bit too consumed by thoughts of Legs to think of Jack.

Yet Legs had asked him if he'd mind a man or woman joining the two of them. It was clear she wanted to experiment.

And that worried him, a little, mostly because he wasn't sure what she really wanted. Did she want him *and* others, or just... others?

Silence was not an exemplar of manhood, being small and slight. He was as tall as Legs, but wasn't sure he'd get much taller. There were bigger, stronger, and more experienced men out there... or women... if that's what she desired. And if she wanted someone else instead of him... he'd be heartbroken, but he'd try to move on. And *if* that day came, he could do worse than the man before him.

But he wasn't there yet. He needed to talk to Legs first. He was — mostly — certain she loved him and wished to stay with him. If so, then he'd need to figure out if he was good with others joining them. Perhaps, if Jack wished to... Silence might be well with that. He'd have to see what Legs had in mind.

Perhaps he'd make an effort to find her, while he was in the capital. He was growing more and more impatient to be away and closer to her. He needed to speak to her, find out what she wanted, if it was indeed him or...

"When do we leave?" he asked.

"That's the spirit," Jack said rising and striking a bit of a pose. Silence suspected the way Jack was standing was meant to show him off in all his glory. And he was certainly a... taller and larger man than Silence. "We'll head out tomorrow late in the day and stop at Grovner's Green to rest." He grinned. "There, we'll pull a bit of a switch, just in case anyone happens to be watching us."

Silence raised a brow at that, putting his tray aside. Jack kindly picked it up to take with him.

"You'll see," Jack said with another flirtatious wink and turned to leave.

And Silence did see. The next evening Silence, Jack, and Foggy all went to a tavern in Grovner's Green. Jack encouraged Silence and Foggy to drink heartily, or at least look like they were doing so. They then all piled into their carriage and headed back toward Hedgewild in the wee hours of the next morning after having "partied" all night. However, the three of them departed the carriage outside the town and circled back to a farmer's barn, where a wagon had been stowed. Along with the wagon were some new clothes for them. Jack traded in his Noble's finery for home-spun rough cloth. Silence was a bit surprised to find himself in a simple dress. "I'm a farmer, you're my daughter or young wife, your choice. Depends if you want to share my bed or not," Jack said with a wink. Foggy became a beetle and stowed himself among the many bundles in the wagon. They headed out as dawn broke. To any who saw them, they'd be a couple instead of three men, on a wagon instead of a carriage.

Their clandestine mission had begun.

CHAPTER 8

ALVERE

THE CORONATION WAS DONE IN PRIVATE. PRINCE ALVERE became King Alvere the Third. Publicly it was being put out that the prince was dead or missing, and the next in line, a cousin to the prince, named Pierre was being sought. Letters on pigeons had been dispatched already to Pierre, telling him he'd also be crowned in the coming days, as a decoy. Pierre had accepted the dangerous job as symbolic figure-head of the country, so the prince could rule in secret.

After the coronation the prince retired to his new rooms within the palace, a simple suite for a visiting noble and family. There he put the crown in a small, padded chest and locked it with a key, which would remain around his neck.

"I'm now Alain," he said to Fin, who'd waited in the rooms while he'd been crowned. "A simple young noble-man, who will counsel the new king on the war."

"Do you think the ruse will work?" Fin asked. The large man paced, the constant activity seeming odd for a man of his bulk. Then Alvere remembered that in his other form, Fin was a whale, and they never stopped moving, despite their immense size.

"For a while at least." Alvere slumped into a padded chair. He needed to gather his things and be on his way to the warfront by the end of the day, but he could sit here for a moment.

He sighed. "Too many people know the truth for the secret to last more than a few weeks. I think the best we can hope for is to keep ahead of the news and be away from here quickly."

"And you're sure it's safe for you to go to the front?" Fin asked.

"I won't be that close, but I'll need to speak with the Fey. Their treaty is with myself and my family, not the kingdom." Still, Alvere was touched by the man's concern. In the short while they'd known each other, the two had become close. Fin went everywhere the prince did, always around in case the prince needed to make a quick escape... or return to Hedgewild, which was quickly becoming his second home.

Thoughts of Hedgewild were dangerous, though... they led to thoughts of Legs. He took a moment to close his eyes and picture her: wavy, golden-brown hair and large, russet-brown eyes. He recalled the softness and sweetness of her full lips and his imagined gaze traced down to her slender chin and that long neck.

Since he'd left, his mind always pictured her in that loose red-gold outfit. It was what he'd seen her in last. He loved the way it fell over her full breasts, like a silken waterfall, and how the skirt hugged her hips, low slung and sensual, dancing around those amazing, long legs of hers. He recalled the feel of her smooth skin, where he'd touched her hip and back.

He had to push the image away, lest he be overcome with desire for her. Shuddering a sigh, he drew his mind back to his immediate task.

Sitting straighter in his chair, he shifted positions to try to make his pants — which were suddenly very tight and constricting — a bit more comfortable. "From what I've been told, everything on our side is ready for a push to reclaim the lands taken by..." *your people*. That wasn't fair. Fin and House Maverick had no part in the war. "...the rogue Elistans. But the spring has been wet up there, and the conditions are not good at the moment. We'll wait and guard our borders, which will also give us time to reinforce our position. I want to walk among the troops and get a sense for their take on the coming battle. And, of course, talk to the Fey."

Fin stopped his pacing and turned, looking at the prince, with a grin. "You're part Fey, aren't you?"

Alvere had a moment of stunned shock, but now that his secret was out, saw no need to deny it. "Yes, though please do not make that common knowledge." He hung his head a little. "I loved my mother, the woman who raised me." He recalled her flowing blond hair and cheery blue eyes. He missed her and his father. "And I wouldn't want to bring any shame upon her or her family... because she wasn't the woman to whom I was born." He looked up at Fin. "How did you know?"

"I know a half-Fey," he said, tone a bit cautious and guarded. "She too wishes for her secret to remain unknown. But you look a lot like her: shorter than most, with that raven-black hair of yours. From what I understood your father was a large man, and your mother tall and blond, yet you are neither of those things." Fin smiled, a friendly grin. "No need to worry, your secret is safe with me."

Alvere nodded. He hoped everyone else wasn't as astute as this man. It had been a bargain struck by his father. Vauphan had watched the growth of the Lumani magics through Elista for the last several hundred years and feared that power. They had wanted something of their own. So, they'd made a pact with the Fey. He had lain with one of their women, and she had born him a child, the royal heir. The queen, his mother, had known of course and though she had not been fond of her husband being with another, had seen the practicality of the bargain. She'd gone into seclusion for her supposed pregnancy — in the North no less — and returned with him bundled in her arms. And to her credit, she had raised him like her own, loved him and cared for him as a mother should.

Yet, there was something Fin had said which stuck in Alvere's mind. "You know another half-Fey? In Elista?"

Fin laughed. "Just as I would for you, I will say little of her. I may have said too much already."

The prince nodded at that. He was intrigued that a half-Fey might have been born to an Elistan. The Fey lived in small, hard-to-find, communities in the northeastern hills and forest. That was no-where near the Elistan border. Perhaps there were some who roamed as far west as North Elista? He didn't know, yet it seemed odd and unlikely.

The Fey had been driven out of the Far North long ago by some mystical catastrophe, which had made the Shattered Lands. Those forsaken lands were close to the north of Elista and Alvere didn't think many Fey wished to be anywhere near the place. So, he was very intrigued by this mystery person Fin knew.

But he had other, much more important things to worry about. "Are you sure you'll be well, traveling by land for the next week or so?" he asked Fin. Fin was able to transport himself, and anyone with him, instantly from place to place, but only to places he knew, and he'd never been to the north of Vauphan. It would be a long journey in wagons and on foot, for one used to instant travel, or the deep sea.

Fin sighed and patted his full, round belly. "Maverick's been saying I could stand to lose a few pounds. I'm sure the journey will do me some good."

Alvere gave a breath of a laugh and nodded. "Do you have all your things?"

Fin shrugged. "Yes... and no? I don't travel with much. I can always slip back to Hedgewild to get anything I need."

"Does that mean you'll get me a warm breakfast every day?" Alvere joked.

"Sure, if you like," Fin said seriously.

Since he wasn't traveling as a prince — no, he was a king now — he'd have only a cold breakfast of hard trail rations like the rest of the men he'd be traveling with. The idea of a warm and savory breakfast was very appealing. Still, he shook his head.

"No Fin, don't worry about it, and if you can, pack what you'll need for the trip and bring it with you. I don't want us to attract too much attention from the men we'll be traveling with."

Fin nodded. "Understood, I'll pack some things now and return in a moment." And just like that he was gone.

Alvere laughed and rose. He had a little time to himself now and, since bathing would be a luxury during the trip, done in cold rivers most likely, he called for hot water to be brought for a bath.

When it was ready, he sank into the warm embrace of the waters, and closed his eyes again, imagining Legs once more, only this time without that flirty dress...

CHAPTER 9

"IT'S SO GOOD TO SEE YOU!" DOVE SAID, THROWING HER ARMS around me in a tight embrace. My sister — adopted sister in truth — hadn't changed much, still a picture of radiant beauty with her fair skin, pale blond hair, sparkling blue eyes and that stunning hour-glass figure.

While she was hugging me close, she whispered, "I've heard so many odd rumors about you recently."

That sent a shiver down my spine. Not so much her words, but the conspiratorial tone. What had she heard?

I drew back and forced a smile. "We'll have time to talk once I'm settled. Or perhaps we can spend a day shopping in the city. My House Leader gave me a small sum to spend."

Dove took the cue and nodded. "Let's get you settled, then we'll talk." She took my hand and motioned for a servant to grab my few bags, then hurried me up to her room, which was far more lavish than mine at Hedgewild. In fact, it was a small suite. The main room possessed a large sitting area and small dining area. Three doors led to: a small study, a private bathing room with attached privy, and a bedroom with a massive bed and several large wardrobes.

Once we were inside with the doors closed, she said, "The servants will take your things to your room, but come you must be tired from your journey, just relax and sit for a while." She'd been overly loud and the way she glanced at the door made me realize these words were not for me, but for anyone listening in.

Then in a hushed and concerned tone, she asked, "What in The Bloody Pits has been happening in the south?"

We sat, huddled close, on one of the large couches. "Can we talk here?" I whispered.

I was a bit surprised when she hesitated. She leaned in to whisper directly in my ear, voice barely audible even then. "There are those in my House very good at listening in on conversations." Leaning back a little she whispered. "I'd like to think we can talk here, but more and more I'm feeling..." She shivered. "...uncertain about a lot of things."

I nodded. This was interesting indeed. I hadn't been sure what had been happening in the capital, but it seemed there were undertones of mistrust here, which spoke volumes about the state of the nation.

"We're safe to talk here, at least for the moment."

The new voice startled us both, and we turned to see another woman with us in my sister's suite. She was short and slight of build. Her hair reminded me of Alvere's, raven-black and gleaming blue in the bright light coming in through the many windows. Her eyes were emerald green and the similarity of the jewel-toned eyes to the prince's beryl blue was also a bit shocking. She was pale with only a blush of pink on her slender lips. In build, she reminded me a lot of Sparrow. But where Sparrow's demeanor was open and bright, this woman was mysterious and dark. She smiled disarmingly at us.

"Hello Legs, I'm Midnight."

It took me a moment to register those words.

"Oh! Midnight!" I turned to my sister. "We can trust her." Though it occurred to me then, that I was just going off this woman's word that she was who she said she was and turned back to her. "How do we know you're you?"

"Maverick said I'd give you something, yes?"

Right!

That had been set up in advance: there would be a sign so I'd know Midnight was around and watching me. She would leave small green stones, smoothed to be perfectly round, in various places where I could see them to let me know she was there, even if I couldn't see her.

She extended a small hand, delicate fingers closed over the palm. She opened it to reveal a handful of such stones.

I nodded in relief. She put the stones away, somewhere under the all-encompassing black cloak she was wearing and drew in close to the back of the couch, leaning over it to be closer to us. "I am exceptionally good at determining if others are around and listening. But I hear you are too, Legs. You have a spider's sense?"

I did!

Why did I always forget these things?

It's been a long trip and you're tired. Also, Midnight just surprised you and I think you're a little off-kilter. Don't worry, I'll remind you of anything else you've forgotten.

Thanks, Auwei.

I drew in a breath and let my hairs prick up, to feel for any other noises or presences around me. I felt the disturbance in the air of the two women with me... but nothing else... no, wait. Someone passed by in the hall. But they walked past Dove's room without stopping. "Yes, I think we're alone."

"You two are a pair," Dove said, voice hushed. Then to Midnight. "How long have you been in my rooms?"

Midnight smiled a small, mysterious grin. "You don't want to know."

Dove's eyes widened at that, but she settled quickly. "Will one of you tell me what's going on?" she whispered.

I looked to Midnight. "I think you know more than I do."

Midnight came around the couch to sit beside me. I slid closer to Dove as the three of us all leaned in to speak quietly.

"I have been secretly working in the capital for over a year now, listening in on many conversations in many Noble Houses, and all I can say for certain is that... something odd is happening." She looked at me for a long moment, and I felt like I understood this intent gaze.

"Yes, you can tell her," I said.

Midnight nodded. "Someone or something is making it so that when certain Nobles die, their Lumani die with them."

Dove gasped. I'd known this for some time, and it was still a bit shocking. Lumani were immortal. They were not necessarily immune to harm, but it had been thought that the only things that could harm them were in the Mistlands, while they were in their energy form, not while they were True-Bonded to a human.

"Exactly," Midnight said. "We thought this the work of certain Nobles at first. Then, when we discovered the mist-weaver, we—"

"Mistweaver!" Dove gasped again.

"Oh, yes," I said casually. "There was a mistweaver about. She was trying to kill me — in fact she's the one who sent those assassins after me at Silverveil — but don't worry, I killed her."

Dove just gaped at me, and I couldn't help a bit of an internal laugh. It did sound preposterous.

You're really loving this, aren't you?

Just a bit, yeah.

Auwei laughed.

It took Dove a long moment to say, "You're... serious?"

We both nodded.

Dove's wide-eyed shock remained as she looked away for a long moment. "So that's what happened in the South? We heard reports of an attack on your House, but not much more."

"There is a lot more, and I'll fill you in once Midnight has done her bit."

Dove nodded slowly, still stunned as Midnight went on. "I am certain the death of the Lumani is not the work of that mistweaver, since there were a couple deaths while she was rumored to be elsewhere and one confirmed Lumani death since the mistweaver's passing. This means one of two things, neither of which are good. Either there is a second mistweaver, or it is the Nobles themselves who have found a way to kill Lumani. Given the existence of spirit-gifts, that cannot be ruled out."

Dove blinked. "Is that how you remained unnoticed here?" she asked. "A spirit-gift? A couple members of my House possess such abilities."

"Indeed," Midnight said, though she did not elaborate. "What I know is this: first, this cannot be the work of one House. Those killed have been among nearly all the Houses, and given how far reaching these plots are, I can't imagine any one House doing all of this. Second, the Royal House must be involved. Perhaps this goes all the way to the queen, though I haven't confirmed that. But to cover everything up, they would have to be involved at some level. Third, there must be either some code these conspirators use when they speak, or they only talk of such things in the closest and most secret of confines, since I have not been able to determine any confirmed source of these deeds. I have several suspects, that I will not disclose just yet, mostly because I cannot confirm their involvement." She sighed. "It has been a trying year."

"What about the war?" I said.

"War?" Dove whispered. "So Vauphan *is* planning war? Perhaps *they* are behind this? That would make sense. They've sent agents to corrupt members of our Nobility, inciting this internal strife while they attack from without?"

Both of us looked at her.

"No, Dove," I said softly. "Vauphan is not involved. They are planning for war, but only because Elista has already annexed several of their northern provinces."

Dove blinked, shocked again. "What?"

Midnight nodded. "We believe whoever is behind these Lumani deaths is also quietly waging a war in the North. The two things are so grand in nature they couldn't both be happening in secret by *different* parties. It must be a single plot."

"*We* started the war?" Dove asked. "But then..." She seemed confused.

"What?" I asked, prompting her.

"Then why are we only hearing now that we're sending troops to the front? It's all the news around the capital. Most of the standing army and several members from Noble Houses are massing to go north, but that's in response to the threat of a Vauphan invasion, or so we were told."

That was interesting. I looked at Midnight, who nodded.

Dove went on. "But you're saying we started the war? If

so... then we're just using Vauphan as an excuse to mass more troops, probably to take more land?"

"That seems likely," I said. "In truth, the war's been going on for three years now, from what we've heard."

"From who?" she asked.

"From Vauphan. I... we... happen to know the prince of Vauphan and believe his account of events. He is a good man just trying to protect his people."

Dove sat back heavily, shaking her head. "I never imagined..." I could understand her stunned dismay. It was a lot to learn. She turned back to me. "And you killed a mistweaver?"

"I nearly died doing it, but yes."

"You nearly died? I heard you were hurt fighting pirates, was that—?"

"That was the first time she tried to kill me. The second time was in the palace at Vauphan, when she succeeded in killing the king and queen. Probably to further destabilize their government so we could claim more lands."

Dove just stared at me, blinking slowly.

Midnight took that opportunity to speak to me. "I'll be close, watching over you. Watch for the signs. I should go now. I don't like to remain out in the open for too long."

I nodded and started a bit when she just vanished from next to me. For a moment, I wondered if she jumped from place to place, like Fin. But no, that's not what I'd been told about her spirit-gift. Hers was around stealth, which meant she was still here, just... imperceptible. I thanked her inwardly and turned back to Dove.

"Where did she go?" Dove asked.

"She's still here. She's keeping an eye on me, since someone out there still wants me dead."

"Dead?" Dove's voice rose an octave. She was having a harder and harder time with these realizations.

I nodded. "There was a prophesy or foretelling or future-seeing or something. Someone, maybe a mistweaver, saw that I'd get in the way of all these plans and potentially stop them. So, they're trying to kill me, whoever *they* are."

"Oh, sister! That's horrible. Why..." Her mouth worked for a moment with no words. Then she nodded. "Of course you couldn't tell me any of this. You probably suspected any correspondence would be spied upon or something." She leaned over and embraced me tightly. "Oh, Legs, I'm so sorry you had to go through all of this. It's just horrible! I'm here for anything you might need."

That was the best news I'd heard in a long time.

CHAPTER 10

THE NEXT DAY DOVE AND I WENT FOR A CARRIAGE RIDE, leaving the city. Dove knew of some paths through light forest along the edge of the Elis River. We walked for some time, leaving the carriage far behind, before we spoke freely once again.

Dove sighed heavily. "I have to admit, all this talk of conspiracies and secret cabals within the Noble Houses is terrifying! And you... They're trying to kill you! How can you remain so calm? I hardly slept a wink last night."

I smiled, though it had a distinctly sad tinge to it. "I'm sorry to drag you into this, sis."

"You're sorry to drag me...?" She gaped at me. "I don't know how you've done this on your own for as long as you have."

"I'm not on my own," I said, sure and confident, if not happy about the situation. "I have Auwei and my Noble House. They've protected me, helping me through all of this."

"I'm glad you have them." She seemed to deflate a little.

"I have a few friends in my House, but most of our members came from Noble parents. They're..."

"Distant, stuck-up, annoying bastards?" I supplied.

She laughed. "Not all at once no, but yeah. Some are distant, some treat me like I'm less than them because I came from 'normal folk,' some ignore me all together. There are forty-seven members of Pegasus House, and I can count on one hand those I'd consider a friend."

She shook her head. "And as for those I'd trust with my life... or your secret..." Her head just kept shaking to provide her thoughts on that matter. "It feels... cold, here in the capital," she said, voice trailing into melancholy. "The sad truth is, it wouldn't surprise me if members of my House were a part of this plot. I don't even know what half of the House is doing. A third of our members are generally not in the capital at any given time. And there are a few that I've still never met, after four years here." She looked at me and smiled. "You should count yourself lucky your House is small and close. It must feel more... like a family."

I grieved for the loss I heard in her voice. "I'm still your family. And you can come visit my new family any time you'd like. They'd welcome you with open arms."

She gave a tremulous smile at that, and I realized I'd only emphasized the comfort of my House compared to hers. "I'm sorry."

"No, don't be. I'm glad you found a home." She took my hand and held it tightly as we walked. She changed the topic: "Are there any boys you're seeing?"

Well, there was Silence...

...And a new lady friend...

...And the prince of Vauphan...

"That's... complicated."

Her eyes went wide, latching onto this diversion. "Oh! That sounds interesting. You have to tell me everything!"

So I did, remembering to keep my voice low and use my spider-sense to discern if there was anyone else around.

Oddly I did sense one other person around, and that... comforted me. Midnight was still nearby.

Dove gasped in all the right places as I told her of my lovers. There was wide-eyed, stunned silence when I spoke of the prince. And she gaped, all curious wonder, when I spoke of Sparrow.

"You *have* been busy and... adventurous, haven't you!" She elbowed me softly, shaking her head. "It shouldn't surprise me though. You were always more adventurous than I."

We walked in silence for a while and the mood slowly shifted from bright to gloomy once more. "Is there... anything I can do to help?" Dove asked after a while.

"You're doing it," I said and took up her hand again to squeeze it. "Just being here for me." Though... "And... if there is anything odd you hear from yours or other Noble Houses...?" I left that open.

She nodded.

After a moment, she asked, "I'm assuming you heard about the queen?"

"The queen? No. What happened?"

"Oh... well, she's gone into seclusion; shut herself away. Apparently, she needed some time to recuperate from... something? It's unclear whether she had an illness or just became overwhelmed from running the nation. Others in her House are handling the affairs of state. I assumed you would have heard."

I shook my head. "No. This is news to me." But did it mean anything? I had no clue. I looked around for

Midnight, but she didn't make an appearance to add anything. "So, we're sending armies north, and the queen is indisposed. That certainly adds... something to all the oddities going on. I just wish we knew who was behind all this and what their ultimate plan was."

Dove nodded.

"The other thing I'm to do while I'm here, supposedly vacationing with you, is to be seen. I'm to go to balls and social events and keep my ears open for any strange rumors. Any thoughts for where to go?"

"There's a ball tonight at Lady Vicuna's estates. I don't know if anyone important is going to be there, or if there will be any talk of intrigue. It's supposed to be for the young eligible Nobles to go and meet and mingle."

"Well, we are both young and eligible," I said with a grin.

"Well, actually...?"

"No!" I gasped. "You're seeing someone?"

She flushed, grinned, then shrugged. "His name is Lord Hale. He's Lord Horn's son, but he's not in our House. He's actually in the Royal House."

It was my turn to gape. "You're dating a Royal? And from his name he certainly sounds buff and... healthy."

Her blush deepened. "He's a complete gentleman and... we haven't been... together yet, but—" A sensuous shiver ran through her. "He *is* big and so very strong. When he holds me close, I practically melt!"

"What's his avatar?"

She grinned. "A gorilla."

I nodded. "I'm happy for you. Will he be at this party tonight?"

"Only if I go and ask him to come."

"Will you?"

She nodded. "Sure, let's go and have some fun and forget

about all this horridness, and you can meet Hale and size him up for yourself," she teased, then, with a mock scolding tone, added, "But don't you dare try to steal him!"

"From you? How? You've always outshined me!"

She grimaced. "You still can't see it, can you?"

"See what?" I asked. "Your amazing beauty and grace and poise. I've always seen that."

She laughed, then grew serious. "I may have all those things, but you've always had a... presence about you, Legs. People are drawn to you."

"Oh?" Though now that I thought about it, perhaps that had something to do with what Auwei was always going on about: my sometimes power of spirit.

It's nothing to mock. It's there, and your sister is right. You do have a presence. You may not be the most objectively beautiful woman in the room, but eyes are still drawn to you. I've noticed it, even if you haven't.

Oh...

"I'll keep my hands off him, don't you worry," I said. "He's all yours." I still couldn't believe it. "A Royal!"

"I know!"

And we giggled together as she told me more about him.

We returned to the city for lunch, and Dove sent a message to her guy saying she wished to meet him at this ball. Then, we spent the afternoon shopping for a gown for me. We settled on a flowing affair of crimson silk, which looked amazing on me. It even had an exposed mid-section, which was perfect. The top was form-fitting silk brocade with a golden-threaded pattern over the underlying crimson. It clung to my chest and arms, with long sleeves, showing off the needlework. A swath of material then ran down from below the chest, twisting around the left side to above the buttocks all along the back, leaving my belly and right side uncovered. The skirts were waves of silk, with trimmings of brocade at the hem and over the lower back of the dress, over my buttocks.

One of Dove's friends, a longtime member of Pegasus House named Lady Willow, helped me with my makeup and hair, which I was not used to doing, while Dove got ready. She, of course, was stunning in white, with her fair skin, hour-glass figure, blue eyes and pale-blond hair. As much as I thought I looked good in my dress, I still couldn't imagine anyone seeing anything but her at this party.

We took a carriage across town to a massive estate, the sprawling four-story manor house seemed somehow small amidst the lavish gardens on the extensive plot of land at the edge of the capital.

I still cringed a little when the herald announced me as "Lady Legs."

And I was right, people did look my way, but far more looked when Dove was announced. I probably imagined it, but I even thought a hush fell over the crowd as they took in her beauty.

Then a massive form came out of the shadows, and I nearly jumped out of my skin. But he went to Dove, and she threw herself into his arms... and wow what arms they were. If this was Hale — and by Dove's reaction it certainly seemed to be — he was a sight indeed. He was taller than Ant by half a head, but just as massively built. The pale-blue silken fabric of his shirt strained over huge shoulders and thick arms. Though it was the massiveness of his forearms which stunned me, nearly as big as my head! He had to pick Dove up to kiss her, but that didn't seem a challenge at all. He had a bull neck, with a thick mane of blond hair and striking amethyst eyes.

"Legs, this is Hale!" Dove said, once she'd been set down.

She was just a bit breathless from the passion of the kiss he'd laid upon her, and in public no less.

He turned to me, and those violet eyes looked me over. He extended a meaty hand, easily three times the size of mine and smiled. "A pleasure to meet you. Dove has told me so much about you." There was something in his dark gaze, a feral hunger. I suddenly felt like prey cornered by a predator.

"The pleasure is mine," I said with a bit of a curtsy... though I really had no idea how to curtsy. *I should learn.*

He raised my hand to his lips, but didn't actually kiss it. Just a motion of respect. Then his gaze was back on Dove, and I felt freed and lighter.

Wow, that is an intense man.

Agreed, Auwei said in awe.

He swept Dove easily into his arms, like she was weightless, and carried her the rest of the way into the large hall, as she laughed and playfully beat on his massive chest to be put down. He finally knelt and set her gently on the floor before asking for a dance. They swirled into the crowd of dancers and I was left alone. With Hale's size though, it was easy enough to keep tabs on him.

"I sense danger in him," Midnight whispered in my ear, and I nearly jumped to the high-vaulted ceiling. When I looked, she wasn't there, of course.

"Oh?" I whispered. "You don't say. Danger other than the fact that he could casually snap me like a twig?"

A soft chuckle. "There is that, but yes, something more."

And he was dating my sister. Great.

"I'm going to mingle and listen in. I'm assuming you'll do the same?"

"Yes, but I'll try to remain close."

Then she was gone. It only occurred to me at that point,

that I'd sensed her presence — and been comforted by it — even if I hadn't seen her around. Apparently, I was getting the hang of using my avatar abilities all the time.

"Might I have this dance?"

I turned to the voice and was surprised to see Creek standing there. He'd been my height back at Silverveil but was now a half-head taller and had filled out rather splendidly. His golden hair was perfectly styled, those dark eyes sparkling as he smiled at me. He lowered his voice to say, "You look stunning, by the way. You're... one of my biggest regrets from Silverveil."

Regrets?

You turned him down.

Oh, right.

He is handsome though, and might be pleasant to dance with? Auwei suggested. *Perhaps he has news?*

Perhaps, I said to Auwei. The trouble was, I still hadn't had the conversation I'd wanted to have with Silence. He'd been conscious when I'd gone to see him before we left but in no state for that sort of talk. And that meant seeing anyone just felt a little wrong.

"Legs?" Creek asked again.

Spirits, I'd just been standing there like an idiot.

"Creek, it's good to see you."

"It's Cougar now, remember?"

"Right! Sorry."

"Would you like to dance?" he asked again, holding out a hand.

Right, he'd asked that already. I supposed a dance couldn't hurt. And he *was* part of Panther House. They were charged with protecting the North, our border with Vauphan. Perhaps he'd heard something about the war?

"Yes, that would be lovely, thank you." I took his hand and we walked out onto the floor.

It was only as he pressed me close that I remembered I didn't know how to dance.

Still, I moved with him and only stepped on his feet a few times. He didn't seem to mind. He was strong enough to sweep me around, so my feet barely touched the floor.

I declined a second dance, but asked him if he'd share a drink with me and catch up on things. I'd been a bit too dazed and dazzled by the swirling dance to ask him anything.

He brought me a tall glass of pale red wine. I sipped it as he spoke.

"I'm actually heading out tomorrow. I've finished my training and the remaining members of my House are being called to the front." His voice lowered, leaning close. "The Vauphani are threatening war, and I must go valiantly protect our nation." He leaned a little closer, putting an arm around me. "I would hate to be alone the night before I leave for war."

"And I'm sure you won't be," I said casually. "But you won't be with me."

He sighed, shifting away a little. "You've found someone at Maverick House?"

The easy answer was, "Yes." But I quickly changed the subject back to the war. "What do you know about the Vauphani and the war?" I asked, hoping the curiosity in my voice sounded genuine and innocent.

He grimaced. "I'm a junior member of the House, so not much." He shook his head. "But I've heard rumors that Vauphani soldiers, dressed as bandits, have been harrowing our towns along the border for some time, raping and pillaging with abandon."

I raised my brows with genuine surprise. "Truly?" I was certain this wasn't true, but then Auwei said:

Vilifying the enemy is a common tactic in war. Fighting just any other man is hard, but fighting someone you believe is a truly horrible person makes you a hero.

"As I said, it's a rumor, but the members of my House at the front are saying the situation is grim. Vauphan is a large nation and if they bring their full army to bear, we'll be sorely out-numbered. Luckily it will take time for them to do that. And our forces will get there first. Some have said we should hit them with a preemptive strike, while our armies are roughly even, cut down their numbers while they're still amassing their troops."

I nodded, listening in rapt engagement. I truly was astonished and curious about what people here had been told. I had little doubt now that those behind all of this were in positions of power. They had to be, to get armies moving and spread such misinformation so widely.

I thought I might try to seed a little doubt in Cougar's mind. "What if the other side is being told the same things, that we're horrible violent people? What if this is all just a misunderstanding or, a few warmongers who are seeking only glory and don't care about who dies on either side?"

Cougar frowned, then shook his head. "But why?" he asked, his own doubt showing through. "We've had peace with Vauphan for as long as we've both been nations. *We* have no reason to fight them, so *they* must have started this, trying to claim lands from a smaller nation, spreading their power. That must be it."

"But what if it isn't?" I urged again. "What if it was truly bandits preying on border towns and nothing more?" I didn't think that was the case, but since that's the rumor he'd heard I thought I'd play it up. "If they were doing that on both sides of the border, perhaps we're all up in arms against each other for no reason, and it's just a small group of rogue people we need to find and eliminate." I was proud of how I'd turned the bandits into a small group of rogue people. That might be easier for him to accept than them being members of our own Nobility."

He drew in a long breath. "I suppose." And I could see the doubt in his eyes before he looked away. "But what can I do, I'm just a new member to the House."

"Talk to your leader, perhaps—"

He scoffed. "I don't know how things work at Maverick House. You're small, right? You might be able to talk to your leader, but I've never even met Jaguar. He's been north, at the front while I've been training here. There are close to seventy members of Panther House."

"Don't you have a squad captain or something?"

"A sergeant, yes, but she doesn't have a lot of say in things either. She does what those above her tell her to do. Which, up until now, has been 'whip the newbies into shape.'"

Ah.

"Well, just keep that in mind when you get to the front. Maybe there'll be a chance to talk then." I could only hope I'd swayed him a little.

He nodded. "I will." He rose. "It was a pleasure to see you again, Legs." His eyes roamed over me, like he wanted to remember me like this. "But I do not intend to spend tonight alone and I must woo another it seems. Take care." He bowed and moved back toward the crowds near the dance floor.

That's when Dove and Hale found me.

"We're going for a walk in the gardens," Dove said, a bit

breathless and glowing with a hint of perspiration from her dances. "Would you like to come along?"

I shook my head. "You two go, be all romantic. I'll just get in the way."

"No, I'd love to get the chance to know my beautiful Dove's sister," Hale said. He didn't look winded at all. "And the gardens will be quiet, easier to talk."

I shrugged. "Are you certain?" I would have thought he'd want to be alone with Dove.

He nodded. "Yes, please come along."

I rose. "As you wish." I linked arms with Dove. Hale enveloped Dove's other hand in his. And the three of us left the hall, stepping out into the night.

And that's when everything went to The Deepest, Blackest Pits.

CHAPTER 11

IT WAS A WARM SPRING NIGHT BUT COMPARED TO THE HEAT inside, it felt crisp and cool, refreshing. I took a long invigorating breath as we moved out from the dazzling, multicolored light cast from the many windows of the manor.

Hale pulled Dove close, his arm going around her, which pulled her away from me. She leaned against him, head on his massive shoulder as they walked. I was happy she'd found someone.

There were pleasant little lanterns here and there among the sprawling gardens, which allowed passers to enjoy the streams, fountains, and greenery even at night. We walked in silence for some time before Hale spoke.

"I'm dying to know," Hale said with a certain eagerness in his voice. "How you survived a battle with a mistweaver and killed her!"

I was a bit surprised Dove had told him that. She hadn't known herself until the previous day. She must have mentioned it while they'd danced.

"It was harrowing indeed," I said, recalling the events, while not really wanting to recall them. Perhaps I'd just gloss over things. "She'd been sent to kill the king and queen of Vauphan, perhaps to enflame this war between our two nations. But she was also there to kill me."

It wasn't her first time trying either, but I didn't mention that.

"Another of my House was in danger, and there was information he needed to get back to those here in Elista. I had to give him time. In truth, I didn't know if I could fight the mistweaver. She came at me from all sides, using the mists themselves to attack me, but then I figured out how to sense her in the mists. I spun some of my webbing and when she appeared next — though I was half-dead — I managed to cover her mouth and nose with it. She couldn't breathe. Then, while she struggled, I used her own dagger against her." I shivered. Even saying that much was making me tremble and sweat in the night's breeze.

"That easy?" he said with a laugh.

"It wasn't easy at all," I replied. "I was on the brink of death. I only survived because one of my House has a spirit-gift of healing and was close by to help."

"Too bad," Hale said with a sigh.

I was a bit confused. "Too bad?"

He laughed. "Too bad she didn't kill you." He pulled Dove close, his arm having been around her, a meaty hand on her hip. "I was really looking forward to consoling my little Dove here when she got the news. Maybe *then* she'd finally spread her legs for me."

"Hale?" I could see Dove's confusion, trying to pull away from him. "What are you—" The rest was a muffled scream, which only I heard. We'd walked well away from the house, no one else was around as Hale pulled Dove close, one hand over her mouth, the other pinning her against him, her back to his chest. There was panic in her wide eyes as we both caught on too late to what was happening.

"Let her go, you—"

"You don't make the demands, girl," Hale growled. "I'm the one holding your sister's life by a thread. One wrong move or a shout from you and I'll snap her pretty little neck."

I froze, not quite believing what I was hearing, even as I felt something hard and powerful rise inside me.

Oh... I think that's your gift, whatever we're calling it, Auwei said. *But I don't know what to do. Though, why isn't Dove veering?*

I was thinking the same thing. As a bird, she'd have a moment of being much smaller, hopefully enough to fly away. "Dove, you need to—"

"Veer?" Hale sneered with a laugh. "She can't. And neither can you. That's my spirit-gift. I can even cut you off from your Lumani entirely."

That's not possible, is it? I asked Auwei.

Auwei?

Auwei?

But she wasn't there.

I tried veering, but couldn't.

Hale laughed. "I never thought my gift that useful, *until* I was assigned as an assassin. It makes things a lot easier." He grinned at me. "Now, keep quiet and follow me if you want your sister to live," he said, hurrying down the path toward the edges of the estate. We came to a wall with a small gate, meant for pedestrian traffic, not carriages. Perhaps it was a servants' entrance?

"Open that and step out," Hale said to me.

Everything was happening too fast. I needed to free Dove, but I didn't know what to do. I'd fought larger foes before. I could defeat Ant sometimes when sparring, but not every time. And this man was huge and still holding my sister. I couldn't do anything or he'd kill her.

Think! I demanded of my own mind.

I fumbled with the gate for a long moment, not really sure what I was doing before realizing it needed a key and I didn't have one.

"Bash it open," Hale said.

I wanted to say: *you do it*! But instead, I just took all my anger and frustration and planted a nice hard side-kick on the latch area. With a screeching snap, it swung open.

I hoped someone had heard that.

Wait.

"Midnight?" I whispered.

No response.

"What was that?" Hale said. "Never mind. Move out into the lane, now!"

I did.

But I'd only taken half a step when I was grabbed from the side. A large man — though thankfully nowhere near as large as Hale — pulled me into a group of three brutes waiting in the alley. Huts and hovels crowded the lane, a shocking disparity from the riches we'd just left.

I struggled for a moment before Hale was through the gate. "Stop fighting or she dies!" he hissed.

Reluctantly, I did.

Blackened bloody bones in The Deepest Darkest Pits! What could I do?

"Midnight?" I whispered again. But again... nothing.

"No, it's not midnight," Hale hissed, confused. "It's not even— That doesn't matter. Listen up, as I'm only going to say this once. You've escaped death too many times already. You're going to submit and let these men kill you. If you do, you'll die quickly and I'll let Dove go. If you don't, you die painfully and I'll also take my time with my dear little Dove here. I'll do things you can't imagine before she finally dies screaming and alone. So, what will it be?"

Panic consumed me. I didn't want to die, and my spirit-gift wasn't going to let that happen, but I couldn't let my sister die either!

"I submit!" I said, stilling my body. I wasn't submitting, but I needed a moment, needed Hale to think he'd won.

Now Think! I shouted at myself. *How do I get out of this?*

The brute holding my arm pulled me back, so my back was against the wall of the estate. Another brute grabbed my left arm and made sure I wasn't going anywhere as the third pulled out a long knife. My arms were pinned. I could kick that third man to keep him back, but if I did, bad things would happen to Dove. I looked around frantically, hoping Midnight would show up. Instead, what I saw, was not good. A carriage was parked a little way down this lane, dark in the night, but I could see at least two shadowy figures around it.

That's where Hale was heading, still holding Dove, who struggled in vain.

Hale looked away for just a moment as the man with the knife stabbed at my chest.

I reacted on instinct, kicking between my attacker's legs. He grunted and doubled over, but not before sliding the knife into my shoulder. I think he'd been aiming for my heart, but he'd shifted when I'd kicked him.

Pain exploded through my shoulder and, awkwardly, the knife had gone through the hand of one of the men holding me, pinning him to me. He screamed.

I screamed.

Hale turned, his muscles bunching as his grip shifted on

Dove, getting a solid hold on her chin, so he could break her neck.

Then Hale screamed, blood flying as his hands came away from her. Dove fell to the ground limp with fear.

"I'm here now, fight!" I heard Midnight's voice.

Finally!

Pain became a distant thing, whether from my spirit-gift or just because of my fury.

I twisted, kneeing the man holding me — but not pinned to me — in the groin. He released me. With my now free hand, I plucked the knife out of my shoulder, then quickly slashed the throat of the man who had been pinned to me. He fell back, mouth open but no sound coming out as he died.

I grabbed a fistful of hair of the man kneeling in front of me, who'd had the knife initially. Pulling his head up, I sank the knife into his throat, not caring for the carnage I was wreaking. I saw only red, fury blinding me as I turned toward the third man, while Midnight fought Hale.

I would have thought she'd cut him up quickly, but it seemed he was quick for a man of his size and with his long arms he had significant reach over the much smaller Midnight. He had a dagger out and was easily keeping her short sword at bay as he backed toward the carriage. Even if she disappeared, he seemed able to track or predict her movements and though she was able to cut him, none were deep, nor hindering him much. He was truly a frightening foe. Luckily, he'd abandoned Dove, who still sat quivering in the laneway.

"Keep the last one alive!" Midnight called to me.

It took extreme willpower, but I stopped myself from gutting the third man. Instead, I kneed him in the face and he went slack. I tossed the knife away — over the wall into the gardens — and stalked toward Hale.

He saw me coming and bolted, jumping into the carriage as it took off down the alley.

"Let him go!" Midnight called. "Save your sister!"

No, he has to die, now!

No, Legs, stop. If Midnight couldn't take him, I don't think you can, not yet, not now. Tend to your sister, I don't doubt you'll have another chance with him.

Auwei was right. I ground my teeth, but my fury slowly subsided.

Also... *You're Back!_*Relief flooded me now that Auwei and I could communicate again. I had felt like I'd lost a part of me, a large part.

I'm guessing Hale's out of range to block us, she mused, sounding relieved herself.

Thank the Spirits for that.

Dove was not far away, stunned and weeping. I went and knelt next to her, holding her tightly. There was nothing I could say that would make this right. It was clear now that her beau had only been courting her to get to me, and he was very much not what he seemed.

This had all been my fault.

Spirits! When would this madness end?

CHAPTER 12

"WE NEED TO GET YOU AND YOUR SISTER OUT OF THE CITY," Midnight said, all business.

"What we need to do, is kill *that man*," I muttered, low and vicious, hugging Dove's head to my chest.

"No, we need him alive to lead us to whoever's behind all this." Midnight's tone held an edge of excitement. "Don't you see? They finally made a mistake. Our plan worked. Once we *capture* Hale, we can finally get some answers."

"I thought that's what he's for." I nodded my head to the one brute I'd left alive.

"No, he's to lead us to Hale. Then we question Hale."

"Then we kill Hale?"

She sighed, shaking her head. Motioning to my sister, she asked, "Can she walk?" Then as if a side note, she added, "You're bleeding."

Was I?

Yes, your shoulder, but the wound isn't as bad as it should be. I think your gift is already closing it up.

"I'll be fine. I'm a survivor." I rose, helping Dove up, but she was still a mess and not ready to stand. I scooped her into my arms. It was only once I was carrying her, with Midnight looking at me with a hint of surprise, that I realized, I shouldn't have had the strength to do this — especially wounded — and yet I hardly noticed her weight.

I thought we'd established that you were stronger with your spirit-gift. That's how you were able to lower the prince down the cliffs, remember?

Right! But that time I'd been struggling: wounded and exhausted. This... this felt easy.

"Where are we going?" I asked.

Midnight looked around. "I doubt we'll find a carriage in this part of town at this hour. Wait here, and keep an eye on him." She indicated the unconscious brute. Then she veered into a bat and flitted away into the night.

"I guess I can put you down," I said to Dove, though she didn't respond, still probably in shock. I couldn't blame her. Having the man you love — who you thought loved you — betray you in such a horrible way... I couldn't imagine what that must feel like. And it was all because of me. I wouldn't be surprised if, once she had recovered from all of this, she hated me.

I set her down, leaning her against the wall, and stood next to her, keeping an eye out for trouble.

Luckily, I didn't have to wait long before I heard the creaking axles and clopping hooves of a carriage approaching.

My *Hero* gift surged as I prepared for trouble, but it was Midnight in the driver's seat as the carriage drew close. She reined in the two-horse team and hopped down easily. "Get her inside," she said, heading for the brute.

"Where'd you get the carriage from?" I asked.

"Don't ask."

We loaded my sister and the brute into the carriage and were off.

Midnight took us out of the city, into the countryside. I didn't know how long we traveled, but the stars had not shifted much in the sky by the time we turned off the road onto a long laneway. We stopped in front of a low farmhouse and Midnight hopped down from the driver's seat.

"Stay inside. I need to confer with the locals."

She knocked on the door of the farmhouse. A woman answered, though I didn't get a good look at her, then Midnight returned. "Take your sister inside, we're preparing a bed for her. Once she's settled, meet me in the barn." She indicated a second large building. I picked up Dove and went inside, as Midnight dragged the brute toward the barn.

I was greeted at the door by a woman in her middle years with grey in her brown hair and a careworn look in her eyes. She led me to a small room with a simple bed and a chest of drawers, nothing else. I made sure Dove was resting, she'd passed out on the trip here, then went back out to the hallway with the woman.

"Thank you," I said softly. "For giving up your house so easily to us strangers."

She gave a little laugh. "You and I haven't met before, but Midnight is no stranger. I am Ana, Maverick's older sister."

I gaped. Maverick... well of course he could have family like anyone else. And now that I knew, I could see it. The same bronzed complexion and something similar around the eyes and nose. Even the hair, a bit wiry and unkempt. And she was built strong. I'd assumed that was from farm work, and it probably was, but she had a similar sturdiness to Maverick.

"What's your name?" Ana asked. "I'm always delighted to meet members of Maverick's House."

"Legs."

She grinned at that. Then her gaze was drawn to my shoulder. "I have some bandages, let me look at that." I sat at her kitchen table as she retrieved some cloth strips, then she tore away the shoulder and arm of my dress — it was ruined anyway — and bandaged up my shoulder. "It doesn't look that bad," she said. "You'll be able to use that arm again in a couple weeks."

Probably a couple days, knowing my accelerated healing, but I just nodded and thanked her. Then I made my way out to the barn.

Midnight had the brute trussed up, hands bound over his head, hanging on what looked like the stub of a branch protruding from one of the wooden support beams. A lantern was lit and she was just dousing him with a bucket of water as I arrived.

The man sputtered to life, squirming and opening his eyes. He quickly assessed the situation and turned hard. "I ain't tellin' you nothin'," he sneered. "You migh' as well kill me, 'cause those I work for surely will kill me if I tell you anythin'."

I could believe that.

I glanced at Midnight, hoping she'd have more experience with things like this. I surely didn't. She seemed to consider things for a long moment before saying: "What if I could guarantee that you'd live if you tell us just one little thing?"

He quirked a brow in question. "How's that?"

She smiled. "All we want to know is where to find Lord Hale. There are any number of common places he could be, but I'm willing to bet he went to ground, and that you know where that is." I saw him about to answer, but she spoke over him quickly. "And when we find him, we're going to make sure he talks." Her grin was a frightening and feral thing. "And then, no one will be looking for you. They'll be looking for him."

That sounded mostly logical to me.

The man considered for a long moment. "And you'd let me go?"

"Once we have Hale's location, yes." She raised a finger. "But... if you lie to us. I will track you to the ends of your days and make sure your death is slow and painful." And the way she said it, with little emotion and a cold smile, terrified me.

The man hung there, brooding for a long moment. Finally, he spoke: "There's a tavern called the Slippery Eel, down by the river. There're tunnels under there that take you to the Owl House estate, a whole warren of tunnels, easy to get lost, and down there are a few hidey-holes, places to lay low. That's where he'll be, if he hasn't already run home to..." The man seemed to realize he was about to say something he shouldn't and stopped himself. "He'll be down there, somewhere."

Midnight nodded. "Sounds reasonable. She made a movement with her hand and the thing I'd thought was a branch seemed to shrink back into the wooden beam. The brute fell, collapsing to his knees.

What was that? I asked Auwei. *She seemed to manipulate the wood of that beam?*

Fey Magic.

Oh... Right! Maverick had said something about Midnight being half-Fey.

But did that mean...? Prince Alvere looked so much like Midnight, the same dark hair and jewel toned eyes. *Is Alvere half-Fey too?*

It's possible. Those attributes are not always distinctly Fey, but it does suggest a Fey heritage.

Oh...

I returned to myself with a blink. If we were going to let this man go, I wanted to make sure he had something to remember me by. I went over to him and slapped him as hard as I could across the face. My *Hero* gift had faded, so I didn't break his neck, but his head turned and I left an angry red mark. "That's for trying to kill me."

The man shook it off and held out his hands and the bindings around them. I turned from him. "You do it," I said to Midnight. "If you put a knife in my hands, I can't say I won't kill him."

I walked out of the barn into the night. It had grown cooler, or perhaps I'd grown warmer, heated by my own anger at the night's events.

I heard footfalls scampering away out the other side of the barn, then Midnight appeared beside me. I'd known she was coming, using my spider-sense, even if I hadn't heard her footfalls. She was very quiet.

"What now?" I asked. "Searching a warren of tunnels sounds like an easy way to get trapped and killed."

"I'm glad you agree," she said. "For now, we wait. Tomorrow some help should arrive and we can make a plan."

"Help?" I knew Maverick, Amber, and Sparrow were in the city, though I didn't really know what they were doing.

She nodded and said, "Get some sleep, if you can." Then she vanished from beside me.

But... I had so many questions!

Midnight was certainly mysterious... and infuriating.

I went back inside and found Ana at her kitchen table, having made some tea. She offered a cup and I took it. She said nothing, but I needed to talk, so I asked: "How did you get involved in all this?" Though I felt I should clarify: "Other than being Maverick's sister?"

She smiled, looking into her tea, which she held in both hands, letting the steam warm her face. "We were always close, my brother and I, but very different. I had no desire to be Chosen, but it was all he wanted. After he was Chosen, he returned here. He didn't test for Noble right away. He helped out on the farm and discovered what he could do, but even before a year was up, I could tell he was growing restless. So, I told him to go and test; to be more. He grudgingly went and came back elated that he'd been selected. Even then, he returned as often as he could to help out here." She took a sip of her tea and sighed. "Even once he was master of the House, he'd make trips and introduce me to other members. Then he started making it a habit. After he'd selected new members, he'd bring them here, introduce us and make some silly threat that if they misbehaved, he'd send them to help on the farm." She laughed. Then she looked up at me. "He didn't do that with you. Odd."

I thought back and nodded. "He had business in the city. He stayed behind, and it was Lady Crane who took us to Hedgewild."

"Ah, that would explain it. She never liked me much. I'm too raw and blunt for her sensibilities. Anyway, my house has become a bit of a safe haven for his members. Midnight has been in a lot over the past few months. She can't reveal herself in the capital, and when she just needed someone to talk to, she'd come here."

That made sense. "Is it just you?"

She shook her head. "No, my husband Kal, and our newborn, Jacob, are sleeping. We have a four-year-old as well. I moved her in with her father and brother before we brought your sister in."

"I'm sorry to put you out like this."

"No trouble at all." Another sip of tea. "Midnight didn't say what happened, but with you being wounded and your sister looking all pale and weak, I assume it wasn't good. Don't feel compelled to tell me. I don't really want to know what trouble my brother is getting himself into." She grimaced. "And dragging young women like you into."

"I volunteered," I said with a tired smile. "I was bait and I got bitten, it was to be expected. I just wasn't expecting my sister to get so caught up in things."

Ana's gaze filled with concern and a curious fear when she looked at me next. "Is it bad... in the city? Midnight hasn't told me much, but I can figure out a thing or two. Something's happening amongst the Nobles, isn't it?"

I nodded. "Yeah, something is, and it's very bad." I tried to smile, but it was false. "And we're going to stop it."

She looked at me, tight-lipped for a long moment. "But your House is small and there are hundreds of Nobles...?"

"They aren't all against us." Though even as I said those words, I wondered. We were going after a member of the Royal House, the son of an upstanding Nobleman. If that got out... sentiment could very easily turn against us.

Whatever we were going to do next... we'd better be very careful doing it.

CHAPTER 13

I SLEPT ON THE SMALL BED WITH DOVE. WHEN SHE WOKE screaming, I comforted her and made sure she settled again. Neither of us slept well. When daylight came, I was bleary eyed and tired, but Dove still slept. I got up and went out for some fresh air. A thick fog hung heavy over the land, washing me with mist. It was refreshing, and I tried to find some sense of peace in this blanket of vapor.

"Sparrow came in the night."

I jumped at Midnight's voice next to me. I had been too tired and not using my spider-senses.

She chuckled softly. "Sorry."

What had she just said, before that?

Sparrow came last night. Auwei said.

Right, thanks.

"Sparrow?" I asked.

She nodded. "She's out there, scouting, keeping an eye out for the others. The master and Amber will be here around lunch, and hopefully... so will the new arrivals."

I raised a brow.

She smiled. "Jack, Silence, and Foggy are on their way to the capital, in disguise. The plan was for them to stop in here first. Once everyone's here, we'll discuss next steps." She half turned to indicate the nearby carriage. "I returned to the city last night and gathered a few things from your sister's rooms. I didn't know what she might want, but I was sure she wouldn't want to go back. I took what I could, including some of your things. It's all in the trunk on the back of the carriage."

"Thanks," I said, weary.

She put a reassuring hand on my shoulder and smiled. "We'll get this all sorted out, don't worry."

But I was so good at worrying.

"I'm going to keep an eye out," she said and then flew away as a bat.

Had she even slept?

She didn't look tired at all.

Probably a Fey thing. So is the fact that she's older than Maverick but looks your age.

Right. Fey.

I went to the carriage and lifted the trunk. It was heavy, but I lugged it inside. I tried to be quiet as I set it down in Dove's room, then rooted through it to find a simple blouse and skirt. I checked my bandage. The wound was still bleeding, but not in a stabbed-with-a-large-knife sort of way, more of an exceptionally-deep-scratch way. It also hurt like The Black Pits now that my *Hero* gift had worn off. I redid the bandages and changed, taking the bottom of the blouse and tying it up above my belly-button. I wanted to be prepared, just in case.

I went outside again as the sound of hooves drew closer. The fog was clearing, no longer the heavy mists around us, but still low overhead, billowing and ominous.

Maverick and Amber arrived on horseback. A small bird accompanying them quickly became Sparrow.

The small woman ran to me, throwing her arms around me in a tight embrace. "I'm so glad you're well," she said, voice muffled with her face in my shoulder; luckily not my injured one. She pulled back enough to be clear when she spoke next. "When Midnight said you'd been attacked, I was so worried." Her deep, forest-green eyes were filled with concern.

I found myself reaching up to smooth her dark hair as I held her close.

"She's harder to kill than that. A tough one is our Legs," Maverick said swinging down off his horse and grabbing the reins as he came to us. He winked at me, though he too looked concerned. So far, he was the only one who knew about the specifics of my spirit-gift.

I was a bit surprised in the next moment when Sparrow put her arms around my neck and pulled herself up for a kiss, even if a quick and chaste one.

"Do I get a kiss too?" Amber teased as she sauntered by. As always, she looked amazing, even after a ride out from the city.

"I missed you," Sparrow whispered once Amber was gone.

We'd only been apart for two days.

"I missed you too." I kissed her again, this time, lingering a little before leading her inside. "My sister's here, would you like to meet her?" I asked. Though, then I felt compelled to add, "Just... she went through a lot last night and she may be a bit fragile, so go easy on her."

Sparrow nodded, smiling.

I left her in the kitchen and returned to Dove's room.

She was awake, sitting in bed, looking a bit stunned. When I closed the door, she flinched a little.

"Did... did that really happen?" she asked in a quavering voice. Then, as if only just noticing where she was: "Where are we?"

I sat next to her, arm around her to provide comfort. "I'm so sorry," I said with a sigh. "It did happen. And we're safe now at a farm outside the city. I promise I'll get you safely away from here and pay that horrible man back for what he did."

She blinked, confused. "Get me away? But my House... my home is here. I can't..." She trailed off as it sank in. Hale was the son of Lord Horn, who was the second in command of Pegasus House, *her* House. It was possible the older man had known of these machinations the whole time. Even if he didn't, that spoke to how unknowing and ineffectual the other high Nobles were. "Oh, Spirits," she breathed. Then she stood suddenly. "I have things I need to get... I can't just... How...?" she moved toward the door, but then flinched back as if it would attack her... no, not the door, but everything beyond it.

"My friend has already retrieved some of your things," I said. "They're in that trunk. If there is anything else dear to you, let me know and we'll make another trip to get it. But you're staying here."

"Yes, I..." She turned back to me, a lost and desperate look in her eyes. I'd never seen her this disoriented and fragile. "I'll stay." She looked directly at me then. "You'll take care of me, won't you Sara?" It was a testament to her unsteady state that she used my old name.

"I will, Ella. Now come and sit, tell me what you need." She moved listlessly and sat with me on the edge of the bed, listing off a few items she felt she couldn't live without. Yet there was little energy, little life left in her voice.

I searched through the chest and found most of what she'd listed. Then I laid her down to rest again. I brought her some food and helped her eat, and finally she settled down after that.

I left the room feeling drained. It was horrible to see her like this, she was usually so bright and full of life. I swore I'd personally tear out Hale's heart for what he'd done to her.

Midnight took Dove's short list of items to retrieve and was off as a bat once more.

I walked out into the yard. The fog was gone, but heavy clouds hung low, and a light rain had started. I didn't really notice. I was too distracted. I just needed to be out in the fresh air. My clothes soaked through quickly, but still, I just stood there.

"You'll catch a chill, you should come in," Sparrow said tugging on my arm.

I turned to her, then turned back as a wagon wheeled its way off the road onto the farm lane. From this distance it looked like a farmer and his daughter on the wagon. I was instantly on guard until they drew closer and I recognized Jack. For a long moment I wondered if the insatiable flirt had picked up some young woman in his travel here, but then... there was something familiar in that mousy brown hair and how the woman moved as she hopped off the wagon... then came running to me.

Silence?

He threw his arms around me and kissed me fully on the lips, and I was more than just a little confused by this, mostly because... he looked really good as a woman and I was just a little aroused at his disguise.

Foggy came tumbling out of the back of the cart and Jack got down slowly, ambling over to us.

"Do we all get a kiss?" he asked with a wink. Between him and Amber... I was always going to be a little off kilter, I think.

"I like the rain!" Foggy said capering around.

"Then feel free to stay out here, I'm going inside to warm up and dry off." Jack moved passed us.

Silence, still holding me tightly, whispered, "I can't wait for you to warm me up."

I smiled at him, but noticed Sparrow's heavy sigh from the corner of my eye. I reached out to her, pulling her into the embrace with us. "Let's all go in and warm up together." And suddenly the cloud hanging over me had lifted, just a little.

Once everyone was assembled and dried off — and Midnight had returned, thankfully able to get the few things Dove had wanted — we all gathered around the not-large-enough table in Ana's kitchen to discuss our next moves.

Maverick spoke, steely and somber, "Things have happened, and I fear our enemies are moving too fast for us to stop." He sighed. "But we'll do what we can." Looking at Midnight, he nodded. "Midnight will remain here with Foggy, Silence, and Sparrow. They are to watch and learn. We finally have a lead, and—"

"I'm staying too," I said, soft but firm. "I have a certain lord to kill."

Maverick's heavy gaze swung to me. "No, Legs, you don't." And I felt his heat rise, warming the room before it dropped off suddenly and we were all left chilled. "I know you want revenge for your sister, but that's not going to come quickly. First, we need to wait and see who Hale leads us to. If we give him time—"

"If we give them time, they'll ruin this nation and kill even more people!" I blurted and instantly flinched back at the surge of annoyed fire in Maverick's eyes. His jaw twitched and bunched, as he stared me down. "Sorry," I mumbled. "Go on."

He nodded. "I don't like this either, just so we're clear. I have a suspicion Hale might be behind other deaths, even the Lumani deaths, and for that he'll need to pay, but for now we need more information." And only then did I realize that the fire in his eyes, the tense jaw, hadn't been for me. It had been for the necessity of this mission. He wanted Hale dead too. That was something at least.

"Legs, you'll be with me, Amber, and Jack. You've played bait long enough, and we have a lead, so we don't need you here anymore. I know you don't like it, but I think you'll like where we're heading."

He drew in a breath, and I could see he was half-expecting to be interrupted, but I remained quiet, listening. "We'll take your sister to Hedgewild and make sure she's safe, then... the next time the prince and Fin check in... the four of us are heading to the Vauphan war front." He blew out a breath. "It's a longshot, but we need to see if we can meet with the Elistan commanders and talk some sense into them. Stop this war before it starts. And if we can't... then we fight." He gave me a cold grin. "You can work out some of your aggressions and test your battle-readiness."

I felt a little cold at that. "Fighting our own people?"

He nodded. "That gives us all the more incentive to stop it before it comes to that. And make sure as few as possible are killed on either side if it does come to war. Trust me, Legs, we have the harder job here."

I believed him.

"Any questions?" Maverick asked.

"What do we do if we find the leader of these rogue Nobles?" Silence asked softly. "What if it is the queen herself?"

Maverick sighed. "Midnight has my orders around that." He shook his head. "I hope this conspiracy doesn't go that far up." He grimaced. "*Whoever* is involved, we can't just go after them. We'd need the support of other Nobles, other Houses or we'd seem like the betrayers, the criminals in all this. So, part of your mission is also to find out who's *not* involved so we can drum up some support."

Silence nodded.

There were no more questions after that.

"We head out tomorrow morning," Maverick said to me, Jack, and Amber. Then he rose and stepped out into the rain.

Both Sparrow and Silence were looking at me expectantly. I'd be leaving them tomorrow. That meant we had most of a day to kill, and I had a lot of pent-up energy to spend.

CHAPTER 14

MY HEART THUNDERED AS SILENCE AND SPARROW FOLLOWED me out to the barn. The rain had stopped, but the clouds were still low and heavy, making the day gloomy and grey.

I'd asked the two of them out, away from the others, to clear the air and get things straight between us. And getting things straight would be great... if I actually knew what that looked like. My emotions were a tumbling mess of confused desire and friendship.

I was so distracted by my thoughts, I didn't even look for a ladder once inside the barn, I just jumped up to the hay loft and threw down the blanket I'd brought. Then I wondered why it was taking so long for the others to get up here.

Sparrow flew. Silence climbed, actually using the ladder.

I sat on the blanket, the soft hay a cushion beneath me. The others did the same, looking from each other back to me.

"Sooo...?" Silence said, clearly uncertain why we were all here.

Where to start?

Start with what you know. Tell them how you feel, even if it's confused.

I nodded.

"I love you both," I said, taking a moment to look into each of their eyes... soft brown and deep green. "You are dear friends to me and... more. Though I don't know how to quantify that more, or if I need to." I paused for a breath.

How do I tell them about Alvere?

Again, just tell them how you feel, Auwei advised. *They'll understand or they won't, but if you're going to be honest with them, you need to tell them. Then let them be however they're going to be: upset, or angry or accepting or whatever.*

You're so Wise.

I know.

"I am not ready to make a choice," I said softly, looking deeply at each of them. "And, I'll be honest, I hope I don't have to make a choice. I love you both... as well as... others."

"Others?" Sparrow breathed. Then, she seemed to make a connection and nodded. "The prince?"

I nodded in return. "Yes."

"The prince?" Silence said. But he had a quick mind. He must have been told the prince of Vauphan had been visiting, and our nation had no prince so... "The prince of Vauphan? You... love him too? Have you been with him?" There was a shocked — and slightly pained — curiosity in the man's soft voice.

"No... well, not like I've been with both of you. We kissed once, but I couldn't go any further in good conscience without speaking to both of you first." It had been a little more than just one kiss, but most of that "more" had been unrestrained feelings and not true actions.

Silence nodded to that, still seeming a bit distant. Then his brow furrowed and he looked at Sparrow. "You two have...?"

She nodded with a shy smile. When Sparrow spoke, her voice was a flighty thing, like her avatar form. "I'd always been curious about... women, and I love Legs dearly and..." She shrugged. "Now I know how I feel." She looked away from Silence with the whispered addition of: "I still don't know how I feel about men."

"A lot of men can be jerks," Silence said with a grimace.

Sparrow giggled at that.

At first, I was a bit taken aback by the vehemence of Silence's comment, but then I recalled he'd been a thief and lived on the streets for most of his life. I guessed he'd learned a lot of hard lessons.

His voice softened when he said, "But some can be... loving and kind."

I smiled to see the two of them getting along. But then they both looked back to me expectantly. I didn't know what to say, or what they wanted, but finally Sparrow said, "You want to be with both of us... and the prince?"

"I do." That was the truth. I grimaced. "And *maybe* more? I don't know yet. I wouldn't want to be with anyone who doesn't love me like you two do. But if another did...?" I shrugged.

"But you love me? You want to be with me?" Silence asked directly.

"Yes," I said and reached over to take his hand. "I love you dearly, Silence and I will never give you up. You were my first, and if you say you don't want me to be with anyone else—" I looked at Sparrow and she nodded, a bit sorrowful, "—I'd accept that."

"Oh," Silence said and took a moment to consider this. Then he smiled faintly and whispered, "You love me." Then he looked at Sparrow. "And you love others." Then that soft, brown-eyed gaze came to me. "You have... too much love to give. You want to share it with everyone who loves you."

That was an interesting way of putting it. "Yes, I supposed that's it."

"And that includes... the prince of Vauphan?" His voice was just a bit hard.

"Yes, Silence. I... I know his countrymen did not... treat you well." That was a massive understatement. "But the prince is a good man. I hope, when you meet him, you'll see that."

Silence was quiet for a long moment before asking, "And what of us? What if we wanted to be with others, who love us?"

I smiled. "I'd be happy for you." Though I furrowed my brow in thought as I considered this fully. If they were getting all steamy with someone else, would I be well with that?

I think I would be, as long as they were just as steamy with me. Slowly, I smiled. "Yes, I think as long as we are all open with each other and our other lovers and everyone agrees, then... that should work, shouldn't it?"

"I'm not sure I wish to be with others," Sparrow confided. She seemed to think for a moment. "But I would be well with you being with others, as long as they are good to you."

"And as long as I return to you?" I asked. She smiled and nodded. "*And* return to you?" I asked Silence." He smiled.

Then Sparrow surprised me by turning to Silence. "I... would you... I am curious about being with a man, and I think... I would want someone like you; someone who will be gentle."

Silence seemed stunned. He looked at me, and I smiled.

I shrugged. "You're both dear to me. You have my blessing."

He blinked, perhaps surprised, then nodded. Turning back to Sparrow, he smiled. "You too are a dear friend. I can do this for you."

I began to rise. "I'll leave you two in peace, and—"

"No, stay, please," Sparrow whispered, reaching out a hand, even though she was too far away to touch me. "Stay." She looked to Silence, questioning.

He blushed deeply. "Are you... saying... you want me... with both...?" He swallowed hard, eyes going a bit wide.

Spirits of the Mists! He was adorable.

"I'll stay if that's what you both want," I said, a little uncertain about this myself.

They both nodded vigorously.

Ohhhh Boyyyyy.

I seek all manner of new experiences, and this would be new for me, Auwei said a bit excitedly. *I've never been with two others at the same time.*

We were all about to find out what that was like.

It was awkward, at first. Trembling, thick-fumbling fingers worked to undress ourselves and each other.

Sparrow gasped when she saw Silence's more-than-ready erection, swollen and red, twitching with barely restrained excitement. His entire body was flushed a beet-red as he looked between us, everyone exposed and uncertain.

I took control, the other two being a bit less sure of themselves. Also, with the level of arousal I was certain Silence must be feeling I didn't know if he'd be as soft and gentle as Sparrow wanted. So I went to him, laying him back on the blanket.

"Kiss him," I said to Sparrow and she leaned down over him, their hands reached and caressed as they drew close, lips touching. I took Silence's erection in my hand and knelt low, bringing it to my lips.

I heard his drawn-out gasp as he realized what I was doing. The trouble was, I didn't really know what I was doing, only that I'd heard men liked it. I used lips and tongue, bobbing slowly, taking him into my mouth as my hand slowly stroked his shaft.

And Silence did indeed like it. I didn't know if it was the use of my mouth, or this whole experience of being with two women, but his excitement quickly boiled over.

"Legs, yes!" he gasped again. "Sparrow I... oh!" and with that I felt his release hot in my mouth. I maintained my hold on him until he was finished, shuddering and breathing heavily.

Yet I didn't stop. I think he was surprised by that. Certainly, he was quickly aroused again, hardening as I encouraged him back to his full readiness.

Then I left off with him, encouraging them to shift, with Sparrow on her back, and Silence on his side, as they continued to kiss and caress.

It only seemed fair, after giving Silence the pleasure of my lips, to do the same with Sparrow. I kissed her slender thighs, moving inward to her folds. I wanted to make sure she was well aroused so her time with Silence was pleasurable.

I was rewarded, hearing her gasp amidst the other moans and breaths. With lips and tongue and fingers, I helped her grow wet and ready. When she finally gasped, "Yes, now..." I moved away.

Silence moved over her, entering her slowly, gently, and she responded with eyes going wide, chest heaving gulps of air as he pushed himself fully inside her. They moved together for some time until their pace began to quicken. Silence rose, kneeling, pulling Sparrow's hips back as he moved within her.

I laid next to Sparrow, reaching down to play my fingers over the aroused bud of her clit. I slid my other hand under her neck and drew her close, lips to mine.

She rewarded me with grasping, firm hands upon my breasts, kneading them with the urgency of a lover on the verge of release as she gasped into my mouth. Her body tensed, back arching, as she drew back from me to whisper, "Silence, yes, yes!"

His thrusts grew quicker.

I kept a steady caress on Sparrow's clit, watching her writhe and convulse through what seemed like an incredibly intense orgasm. Tremors like waves undulated up and down her body, as her eyes rolled up, head tilting back, mouth agape.

I leaned down to kiss her breasts, flicking an aroused nipple with my tongue. She cried out... far louder than I was used to her being. One of her hands clamped down on the back of my head as she called out again and again before finally going limp, body still trembling.

"Spirits and Sprites!" she gasped when she'd regained her breath. "That was... I never imagined..."

Silence beamed, but I caught how he was still rocking slightly inside her, still a bit tense. He'd not released.

I straddled Sparrow, pressing myself to her and our lips met in playful kisses. With my legs open, around Sparrow, I was presenting Silence with a good view of my sex. He got the hint. I felt his seeking fingers, then the press and pressure of his erection entering me. I simmered with arousal, more than ready after watching these two, especially seeing Sparrow reach such incredible heights of bliss.

I left Sparrow's lips long enough to glance back at Silence and say, "Hard."

I felt his hands on my hips, steadying me as he obliged, thrusting with abandon. He'd been so slow and gentle and caring with Sparrow. He deserved to let loose, and so did I.

Shaken by Silence's relentless thrusts, I could no longer kiss Sparrow without our faces jarring together. But she smiled, levering me up a little, supporting my weight on her hands as she grasped my breasts. That was until she pulled herself up and brought her lips to a nipple. The hand that had been upon that breast sought down between my legs as I'd done with her.

That was it for me. The combined pleasure of Silence's hard thrusts, mixed with Sparrow's grasping lips upon my breasts and her delicate caress of my clit, made me tense and cry out with my own hard orgasm. I felt myself clamp down on Silence's swollen shaft, needing him to release. And with a few more hard lunges I felt his explosion within me and heard his own cries of pleasure.

After that, for some time, we simply lay on the blanket, Silence behind me Sparrow in front, as we all came down from our respective highs.

"What did you think?" I asked Sparrow.

She blushed deeply, which only made her brown skin more beautiful. "I... don't think I would have enjoyed it as much if you hadn't been here." Then softer, "It was perfect. Thank you." And finally, a little louder, "Thank you, Silence."

He laughed, then said, "It was literally my pleasure."

Then, the two of them levered themselves up to kiss over me.

I couldn't help but join in, kissing their cheeks and then their lips, back and forth as we played once again. Something told me, we would be here for a while that afternoon.

CHAPTER 15

I LEFT SILENCE AND SPARROW THE NEXT MORNING AMIDST many mutual tears. The rains had stopped, and it promised to be a clear, sunny day. Yet a brisk wind from the north brought a chill, and I wrapped a cloak tight about myself as we left.

Sometime the previous day, Midnight had returned her stolen carriage and acquired a second wagon. It seemed best to travel incognito, so the five of us would become a family of merchants. Maverick and Amber up front, Jack, Dove and me with our legs dangling off the back.

The wagon had several trunks and chests on it, which could easily have been our "precious cargo" but was nothing more than our belongings.

I held Dove close. She'd recovered a bit more, glad to have the few things she'd truly treasured from her old residence, but I think everything that had happened still weighed on her.

I was a hot and cold confusion of emotions. There was sorrow for my sister, and sadness at leaving my dear friends, while I was also warmed by the memory of our precious time together. Then, there was my simmering rage for Lord Hale. I vowed revenge upon him, even if that wouldn't happen any time soon.

"You're shivering. Are you cold?" Dove asked, concerned.

I was cold, but I wasn't shivering because of that. I trembled in rage, recalling that devil of a man.

"No, I'm well." I hugged her closer and she leaned her head on my shoulder.

Jack shifted, leaning against the side of the wagon, one leg up, one leg over the back, looking at us. His tone was serious when he said, "Tonight, we're sparring. You're going to remind me how good you are with a sword before we head to a war zone."

"War zone?" Dove said, confused and frightened.

I glared at Jack and hushed her. "I'll tell you everything later, rest for now."

Luckily, she did. It was a testament to all she'd been through how easily she settled down. But Jack wasn't wrong. I'd fought the mistweaver one on one, but never been in a large-scale battle. I'd never been amidst the chaos of war. I nodded to him, and he nodded back. I'd need to be well prepared for what was to come.

That evening, when Jack and I began to spar, I was surprised that Dove wished to practice as well. Luckily, one of the trunks with us was a chest full of weapons. Jack selected twin dueling blades, I took a rapier and parrying dagger, and Dove took a longsword, one with a long grip, enough for two hands. We thought we'd be doing two on one against Jack, until Maverick stepped in as well. He joined with his thick-bladed arming sword and a large shield. He proposed a different "game." Each of us would attack one person while defending from another. One tap from the flat of the blade and you were out. I had Maverick attacking me while I attacked Jack. Dove attacked Maverick while defending against Jack. I didn't know which of us had it worse.

I quickly realized my little parrying dagger wouldn't be much use against that heavy arming sword Maverick wielded. So... I threw it at him, offhand and awkward. He blocked with his shield, though that left Dove an opening. She, however, was preoccupied simply defending against the onslaught of two smaller but no-less-deadly swords from Jack.

So... I changed the rules.

The best defense is a good offence, right?

Exactly, Auwei agreed.

So, I left off trying to attack Jack and attacked Maverick. "Smart girl," he said with a grin as he caught on.

I was quicker than Maverick, but not by much; his years of experience made him frighteningly quick with that massive blade of his. And with Dove not attacking — doing everything she could to defend against Jack — he could also defend with his shield. I was surprised when I landed a tap on his calf. Though even more surprised to feel a tap on my back. I spun to see Jack grinning and Dove grimacing and shaking her head.

"You left yourself open," Jack said. "You didn't think I'd attack, even though that's what you were doing yourself." He glanced at Dove. "Your sister is good, but once I didn't have to worry about you attacking, I quickly overwhelmed her with two blades, then turned my attention to you."

I sighed. I'd won and lost.

"Worse," Maverick added in. "Your strike to me would most likely have been debilitating, but not fatal. But Jack's strike to you would have been fatal. You sacrificed your life for a minor wound upon a foe."

I nodded, seeing it all now. "I need two weapons," I said looking at my empty left hand. "Or a shield. That parrying dagger is good against some weapons, but against anything heavy, it's useless."

"Agreed," Jack said. "I use it fighting pirates with cutlasses and sabers, but against a hardened warrior with an arming sword or halberd..." He shook his head. "He looked at his twin rapiers. "Even with these, I need to get out of the way often enough. I trust to the longer reach I have with these when fighting someone with a heavier weapon, unless it's a polearm or claymore."

"Then what would you do?"

Jack grinned. "Leave fighting them to Ant or Maverick and move on to someone else."

Maverick glared at him, clearing his throat. A clear indication that that hadn't been the right answer.

"I'd get in close," Jack said, amending his answer, "where their larger two-handed weapon isn't as useful."

Maverick nodded to that.

I had practiced mostly with the rapier, a little longsword and some staff work with Ant. I was curious. "What weapon am I the best with, when I spar with you?" I asked Jack.

He tilted his head and smiled. "I'm glad you finally asked that."

Yeah, I couldn't believe it had taken me that long to ask either. *What do you think I'm best with?* I asked Auwei.

"The staff," Jack said after a moment of thought.

The staff, Auwei confirmed.

And for a moment I had the two of them talking at me in unison:

"You're also exceptionally strong with your hand-fighting skills, your kicks being your strongest attack."

I think perhaps you are just a little afraid of bladed weapons.

"The staff can be used to augment those attacks, used to propel a kick farther, stronger."

Not that you'd hurt yourself, but the idea of actually cutting open another person... The staff is a devastating weapon, but less... overtly violent.

"You'd also have greater reach than most of the other weapons you've tried and it's good for defense."

It also seems more natural in your hands, it flows with you, where you're just a bit... hesitant and awkward still with a sword.

I stood there hearing both of them and trying to parse the words. Eventually I nodded. "So... a staff then?"

Jack shrugged. "Trouble is, you're not as strong as Ant. In an all-out battle it would be a good weapon for you, but you'd have trouble killing a foe with it outright and leaving live foes behind you is never a good idea."

"Not a staff then? What else would work?" I looked at Dove. She'd seem fairly natural with a longsword in her hands, but she also had three extra years of training on me. "Auwei says she thinks I'm hesitant to kill. That I'm more tentative with bladed weapons because they can cut and kill easier." I shrugged feeling a little disheartened. "Perhaps I shouldn't be going to war after all."

Dove came over to give me a hug. "I don't much like the idea of blades and killing either," she whispered, then she sighed heavily. "For Hale, I'd make an exception, but otherwise, I'm used to cutting up practice dummies and that's not the same thing." A shudder rippled through her. "I don't know how I'd do in a true battle."

She wouldn't have to find out. We'd be leaving her at Hedgewild. Which led to my next thought. "Perhaps you should just leave us both at Hedgewild," I said to the others.

"If that's what you want," Maverick said. He had a look in his eyes though, and I thought I could read it well enough. *I know you'll make a great warrior, if you apply yourself.*

I sighed, releasing Dove and turning to Amber, who was sitting nearby preparing the evening meal. "What weapons do you use?"

"Good-looks and guile," she said without hesitation.

"Those won't help you much in a war," I quipped.

She nodded. "True. So, I bring an assortment. My preferred weapons are dual short swords. They don't have the reach of longer blades, but they're sturdy and can take a hit from anything. It means I have to get in close, and that gets bloody and nasty." She gave a fierce grin. "But that's the way I like it." She shrugged. "I also carry some throwing knives, which can be used up close in a pinch as well. I've been known to use a spear also, if I think I want something with reach." She grimaced. "Trouble with a spear is, sometimes if you're really aggressive in running someone through, you can't get the weapon back. You have to give it up and move on to other weapons."

"She's so beautiful and yet so... nasty," Dove whispered.

I was very aware of that.

"Maybe I could try using a staff or two short swords?" I said with a shrug.

Maverick nodded. "Sure, we'll keep training you and see what you're comfortable with."

So, that evening, after we ate, Dove and I got a lesson in fighting with dual short swords from Amber and the two men. I think I took to it a bit more naturally, but with Dove's extra training she picked it up quickly as well.

Then lanterns were lit and hung off the wagon as the others bedded down, but Maverick and I stayed up to train with the staff. I wanted to see how the staff fared against his heavy arming sword. In the end, it was as I expected. I defended well but had trouble truly stopping him. I managed to swipe his legs out from under him at one point, but I had nothing to follow up with. He'd covered his head and upper torso with this shield. So, I could bash at his legs and such, but nothing that would truly hinder him and he was up again quickly.

When we finished, Maverick suggested, "Perhaps try training with a spear, like Amber. You can use it like a staff, so you'd not be relearning much, but it also has a pointed tip you can use to follow up once you've tripped someone." He shrugged. "Find what works for you, but find it fast, if you're coming with us. This war won't wait for you."

I fell asleep with Maverick's words in my head: *This war won't wait for you*, which led to dreams of battle and death.

Needless to say, I didn't sleep well.

CHAPTER 16

SPARROW

SPARROW SAT IN HER AVATAR FORM, HIDDEN AMIDST THE branches of a tall oak tree, watching the comings and goings of the members of the Royal House, Owl House. She had to be very careful. Many members of Owl House were birds, specifically birds of prey. If they caught sight of her, they might consider her a nice light snack. Hence, her hidden position. The oak tree was just outside the walled estate grounds of Owl House, the manor itself was massive, which it had to be for the nearly one hundred members of that House. Even if it hadn't been the Royal House, Owl would have been a powerful Noble House.

Yet she'd seen nothing untoward in the two days she'd been watching the manor, certainly no signs of Lord Hale in human or avatar form.

Sparrow had always been an odd mix of shy and timid with moments of unsuspecting boldness and bravery. She'd learned it early on. Fearing her father, a fisherman who plied the Austel Ocean, she'd learned to keep quiet. The man had a temper and drunk far too much. Though not physically violent, he'd been prone to savage outbursts, shouting horrible things at his family. Her mother had been a rock, impassive against the storm of her father's emotions. She sat and mended nets and prepared their meals with stoic silence. She was distant, to everyone, including her children, which wasn't much better.

When Sparrow had been old enough, she'd gone for the Choosing and been surprised to find Ahena, her Lumani, the first year. She hadn't known what to do once she'd bonded at Silverveil. She'd heard a few other students were testing for Noble and that sounded interesting, so she'd gone. Again, she'd been surprised to be selected by Maverick. He'd said he saw something in her, a core of something tougher than steel, another surprise.

Her time at Maverick House had brought her out of her shell in slow, small steps, and she'd been made a scout, rarely fighting, but useful by seeing what others couldn't from her high vantage point while flying.

Yet it hadn't been until the arrival of Legs, nearly six years later, that she'd found the courage to truly show herself to another person. And since then, she'd felt a new strength growing inside her, a surety, a confidence.

So, she wasn't too worried if any birds of prey came her way. She was fast and agile as a sparrow. And as a person, she was quick with her little knives. She'd only had to use them a few times in true fights with pirates, and her foes had always seemed just a little surprised when they found themselves stuck and bleeding.

As the day drew to a close, she took flight and returned

to the small apartment she and the others shared in the city. She landed on the window, then flitted inside before resuming her human form. None of the others had returned from their day's scouting, so she quickly prepared a meal for them. Ahena was an excellent cook. She loved to bake but could work with nearly anything. The meal was warm and ready when the others returned.

Yet the news they shared as they ate wasn't good. Sparrow reported no interesting news from the Royal House. Silence and Foggy were working together to explore the warren of tunnels beneath the Slippery Eel that led to the Royal House. They reported seeing many people moving through the tunnels, but they hadn't found Hale yet, nor heard any other indicators of betrayal and subterfuge. Midnight had been within the Royal House, moving carefully. Specifically, she'd been trying to find out more about the queen and her supposed retreat away from society. Yet as much as she could go unseen, she could not get into some areas and had had no luck finding the queen. She wasn't in her royal rooms nor any of the easily accessible parts of the house. Two days, and they still had nothing.

"We need to be patient and persistent," Midnight said stoically. "We'll find something to help the others, I know it."

That night, Sparrow and Silence slept together, holding each other close for comfort, uncertain what the next day would bring.

They all went their separate ways the next day. A spring storm loomed over the capital. High winds and lashing rain meant Sparrow would not be doing much flying. So, she bundled herself up in a heavy oiled cloak and stood across from the Slippery Eel, in the shadows of a dark alley, watching the place.

Understandably, few people were out on the streets, so she stood there for some time, seeing no activity. Though her cloak kept her mostly dry, the shifting winds and driving rains managed to trickle some moisture down within the confines of the garment and she began to feel a chill.

As she was thinking of leaving, a large figure ducked out of the doorway of the Slippery Eel. The massive man looked quickly around before heading off at a quick pace into the rains.

Sparrow didn't know Lord Hale, but this man matched the general description: larger than Ant with thick arms — especially the forearms — and blond hair. She'd caught sight of a few strands of pale hair peeking out from under the cowl of his cloak.

She hesitated only a moment before following him. She slipped from alley to alley, shadow to shadow, keeping the large man in sight through the sheets of rain inundating the city. He'd check behind him every now and then, but that large body of his telegraphed his movements, and when she saw his shoulder shift and twitch, she'd make sure she was safe in an alley or duck for cover.

Whoever this was, he was certain of his destination. He made his way through back streets and dark alleys, a circuitous route, but definitely heading across the city. Sparrow was half-certain of where he was going, and her suspicions were confirmed when he reached the walled compound of Pegasus House. He spoke quickly with a gate guard and was admitted.

Interesting.

She'd not be able to follow beyond this point... unless...

It was difficult but not impossible to fly in such downpours of rain. She'd have to make several trips most likely, but it was important enough to risk. She veered into her sparrow form and asked her Lumani Ahena to lend her strength, then flitted to the top of the wall around the Pegasus compound. She made it there in time to see the large man entering a small side door.

She wasn't certain, but she thought she might know where in the house he was heading. Before Legs had come here, only a few days ago — but seeming like a lifetime — Sparrow had scouted the house and knew where Lady Silvermane's rooms were, as well as Lord Horn's, Hale's father.

She made the quick trip up to a window of Silvermane's room to perch on the large stone sill. Peering within, she found Lord Horn there as well. This wasn't uncommon, since the large protector-knight was usually close by his charge.

And as suspected, the large man she'd been following was admitted a few moments later. This had to be Hale.

Her hearing wasn't as good as Midnight's and the three in the room gathered close, speaking in hushed voices. But Sparrow had learned a few tricks. Her eyes in bird form were keen and she'd learned to read a person's lips from a great distance. And as luck would have it, Hale was the one facing her as he spoke. Yet the other two occasionally got in the way, and she had trouble reading their lips from the sides, so she only got bits of the conversation.

Hale spoke, "...most dire... in danger... madwoman, Maverick has trained as an assassin. I don't *think* she'd hurt her sister, but she's quite crazy so I can't be sure. Even with all my skills I... protect my beloved and... away, killing three men. It's clear now Maverick House is working against Elista, though to what end I do not know."

Sparrow was more than a little shocked at this. The man

was blatantly lying about the events of a few nights ago. Though, what was more worrying was that Silvermane and Horn seemed to believe him wholeheartedly.

"Maverick is... not think him a betrayer..." This from Silvermane. She shook her head. "This is dire news indeed. I am worried for young Dove."

Horn nodded at this.

"There is more," Hale said. "They are conspiring with Vauphan against us."

Well, that part was sort of true, but they only sought to stop the coming war, not betray Elista.

"That woman, Legs has seduced their prince and whispers in his ear encouraging their war."

Silvermane shook her head again. "To what end?"

Hale looked weary and sad, clearly an act. "That I do not know. The queen worries we may have a war on two fronts, that Maverick and his seductress will entice the Vauphani to come ashore in the South, while a smaller force, reinforced by the bedeviled Fey, holds the North. They will have us caught in the middle, fighting on two fronts. That is why..." Horn adjusted his position and blocked Hale for a moment. "... the north and overcome their forces now."

Silvermane was nodding. "What do you need?"

"Your most powerful spirit-gifted to bolster the forces in the North. Also, your portion of the army to march south and take Hedgewild."

A cold shudder ran through Sparrow. She hadn't thought it possible they would march on one of their own Noble Houses, but she'd clearly been wrong. Each of the top five Noble Houses controlled a portion of the army of Elista, a precaution from putting too much power in the hands of whatever House currently held the Royal name. Currently, that meant Panther protected the East, Pterolycus the North, Wyvern the West, Pegasus the South, and Owl the Central Capital Region. Though, Pegasus' army hadn't truly been in the south for some time, remaining close to the capital since there was no great threat upon the lands of Southern Elista. The only threat in the south was pirates, occasionally raiding the coast, and Maverick House dealt with them. But if Pegasus did march south... their army of five thousand men would easily overcome the few Nobles at Hedgewild; it would be a massacre. She wanted to run and tell the others now, but forced herself to remain and see what else she could learn.

"I'll do what I must to free Dove," Silvermane said, jaw firm, eyes cold.

"Finally," Hale said, rising. "Spread word to the other Houses of Maverick's betrayal. None in their House can be trusted." He sighed rolling his heavy shoulders. "And if your army or any other House manages to capture Legs... try to keep her alive. I want to make her pay for what she did."

There were grim faces all around.

Lord Horn said something Sparrow couldn't read, then he escorted his son out. Curious, Sparrow flitted over a few sets of windows to Lord Horn's suite and her suspicions were confirmed when the two entered. Again they spoke quietly, but Sparrow could read both their lips well at this angle.

"I don't like hiding things from my mistress," Horn said. He'd turned away from his son for a moment toward the window, and Sparrow saw his lips clearly. She also saw the pain on his aged and weathered face. "You're certain the queen does not wish her daughter to know?"

Hale was hard. "Yes. She must not know the truth. She

believes this war to be just and we must keep up that façade."

Sparrow was stunned. So, the queen *was* behind the war in the North!

"For the sake of the Mists," Horn said.

"For the sake of the Mists, yes." Hale came and laid a hand on his father's shoulder. "No one likes this, but we're doing what we must." They were both facing the window now, Horn still unable to look at his son.

Horn nodded. "And Maverick?"

"Our plans went awry; we could not get ahold of Legs. As Merlin has seen, Legs will end all of this for us, she must be stopped. And if that means eliminating an entire Noble House." He sighed heavily. "We'll do what we must." Those massive shoulders shrugged. "They are small, some new Noble will easily be able to rebuild the South."

So, Lord Horn was fully aware of what was going on, and a part of the treachery, though, to be fair, he didn't seem to like it much.

And Hales mention of Merlin *seeing* that *Legs will end this* for them, was shocking, but confirmed what Legs had learned from the mistweaver, that one of the conspirators could see the future. That's why they'd been going after Legs to begin with. Merlin was the second-in-command of House Owl, the right hand to the queen. If she had some ability — perhaps a spirit-gift — to see the future, that was dangerous indeed.

Horn nodded again, stoic. "I do not like it..." Then he sighed heavily. "...but we'll do what we must," he repeated what his son had said a moment ago.

"For the Mists," Hale said. Sparrow found it interesting they kept repeating that phrase.

"For the Mists," Horn said with a heavy sigh.

They spoke only of familial matters after that, and Sparrow flew away once Hale had left.

Her heart raced. She needed to tell the others. This was far larger than they'd expected. The entire nation was turning against them.

They needed to get out of the capital and warn the others, now!

CHAPTER 17

Fin popped into the great hall, distracting Amber just at the right moment for me to slip past her guard with my spear. I tapped the long metal tip of the spear on her shoulder, a kill.

"Finally!" I gasped.

Amber eyed the weapon and smiled. "I'd say you only won because I was distracted, but distraction is no excuse. There are many distractions on the battlefield. Good for you. We'll practice more once we're in Vauphan." She carefully pushed the haft of the spear away from her, and I let her, drinking in the praise.

I'd excelled with the spear during the two days of relentless training. Dove had been practicing as well, but between the two of us, I'd been the only one to get past Amber's defenses, though not often. This was only the third time I'd been able to do so.

I put the spear aside and ran over to Fin, but the prince wasn't with him.

The large man looked like he'd lost a little weight, still

barrel-chested and large, but with a little less of himself hanging over other parts.

"Looking good, Fin. Is everything set in the North?" I asked.

He nodded with a smile. "Eager to see your little prince?" he teased.

I think I blushed. I *was* excited. I hadn't seen him in a while. Also, now that I'd talked to Silence and Sparrow, I could do more than just kiss the man... if we got a moment alone.

Fin lowered his voice. "He's excited to see you too." He winked.

That shocked me just a little. I didn't think Alvere was one to share such things, but he and Fin had been together for some time, perhaps they'd formed a bond?

"Now, run and get your things, I'm having a bath and a good meal — I'm sick of trail rations — then we'll be off."

I nodded and ran back to Dove. She and I hurried to my room. She'd mostly recovered from her harrowing ordeal with Hale, but she still hadn't wanted to be too far from me. So she'd stayed in my rooms, sometimes sleeping on my large bed, sometimes on one of the comfortable couches. I had already gathered most of my things in a travel bag, but I quickly checked it.

"Well?" I asked Dove. "What's your decision? You coming?" I looked over at her, that flaxen-blond hair of hers, light and weightless, seemed to float about her as she sat heavily on one of the couches.

"So soon?" she whispered. "I... don't know." Her blue eyes clouded with uncertainty. "I want to be where you are, but the more I practice with you, the more I realize I never want to fight. I... don't think I'd do well in a war zone."

I smiled. "Don't worry, you don't have to come. Fin will be back often enough, and I'll visit." I closed up my bag and went over to sit with her. Putting an arm around her, I pulled her close and gave her a tight, side-long hug. "You'll be safe here."

It was ever-so-slight, but I felt a tremor pulse through her. "I don't know if I'll feel truly safe ever again." She gave me a tight smile, and I could see the pain in those blue eyes. "I don't know how you do it. You're so strong..."

I pulled her closer, both arms around her. I couldn't bear to leave her like this. Sometimes she seemed her old self, and others she seemed so delicate and fragile, like the softest touch would shatter her. "I love you, Dove," I said softly. "Don't worry about anything. Ant and the others will take care of you. Take the time you need to..." I didn't know how to end that sentence: *get back to your old self*? I was beginning to wonder if that was even possible. "You'll be well, I know it." I hugged her tighter and she returned the embrace.

I only knew she was crying when she sniffed and spoke, voice tremulous and valiantly trying to overcome her emotions. "You go be amazing out there. I know you'll change the world," she whispered.

Perhaps I was stronger than her, but I wouldn't have gone that far.

"I'll do my best," I said.

When I didn't move for a while, she pulled back and looked up. There were indeed tears on her cheeks, though they seemed all shed now, eyes clear. "Don't you need to go?"

"Fin said he was going to bathe and eat, and he doesn't eat quickly. I've got time."

She smiled and leaned back into me.

We held each other until it began to get dark. Then I finally released her.

She came down to the great hall with me and indeed Fin was only halfway through a large meal. The others who were going to Vauphan were already there, ready, waiting.

Maverick, Amber, Jack, and I would go. The rest of the House would remain here.

I went to where I'd left my spear and grabbed it. I also put on the sword-belt I'd removed while practicing. I felt comfortable with the spear now, as well as dual short swords. For ranged weapons, I'd been practicing with throwing knives. A bow had a much longer range, but the dozen or so small throwing knives were easier to keep on me and move around with.

As for my squeamishness about blades... that was still an uncertainty. We'd see how my first foray went.

My heart raced for so many reasons as Fin rose from his meal. I'd soon see Alvere again. I'd soon see battle for the first time. I was still a bit worried for Dove. And finally, I'd never been that far from home before.

I kissed Dove good-bye, joined hands with the others, then the world spun and we were in a small clearing at the edge of a forest. Through the sparse trees I could see a large camp in the fields beyond.

"Remember," Fin said. "The prince isn't a prince here. He's a minor noble in command of a small group of men. His name is Alain of Beauval."

We all nodded to this, and Fin led us out of the woods into the camp. We got a few interesting looks as we passed other men sitting around fires and eating in the growing dark of the evening, but no comments. They had no reason to suspect we were Elistan. Also, Fin had become well known to many of these men as a retainer to the young "Alain of Beauval."

Fin took us to a large pavilion and entered. No men guarded the tent. The prince was on his own here, trusting to secrecy to keep him safe.

There was a large front room to the tent with carpeting covering the grasses in several places creating areas for sitting and dining. Alvere was leaning over the long dining table, studying some papers. He looked up and a wide grin spread on his face as his gaze met mine. I saw his eyes go wide, his chest fill with a heavy breath.

"Welcome!" he said to us and motioned to several flaps leading to areas in the back of the tent. "Feel free to put your things in the rooms at the back. The one in the middle is mine." He was looking directly at me for that last bit. The suggestion was clear, if I wished to share his room, I was welcome to.

I didn't hesitate in taking my things through the central flap, ignoring some of the looks from the others. There were four other rooms, two on either side of Alvere's, so one for each of the others.

Once inside the "bedroom" I felt myself grow warm. I was really doing this. Committing to sharing a bed with him. It wasn't a large bed, but certainly large for a camp far from civilization. I put my stuff down and went to run my hand over the thick canvas wall. We'd have to be quiet so as not to disturb the others. I hoped I could manage that.

I returned to the living area as the prince poured some tea into five small metal cups.

"Now," he said sitting, as we all did the same. "Let me update you on the situation here at the front." He sighed. "At the moment, Vauphan has the advantage. We have six thousand warriors plus another roughly two hundred Fey, each of which is worth a dozen men."

This was news. I'd known the Fey were to be helping in the war effort, but I hadn't known they were *that* good. I wasn't sure if his comment was hyperbole or not. If not, that small group would be significant indeed. "On the Elistan side, nearly the full complement of Panther House is here, with their five thousand men. On that side, it is the Lumani which are the unknown factor for us. Panther has upwards of fifty members, all with the ability to become hunting cats or other predators. That is not insignificant." He didn't really need to tell us that. "Both sides are expecting reinforcements in the next few days. Vauphan will have two thousand more men by the end of the week and Elista roughly the same... part of the Pterolycus army has been diverted from what we've heard."

How he knew all of this was a mystery to me.

"And the more time passes, the more forces will arrive. I don't know how many more from Elista, but I'd suspect at least another five thousand or so army men and perhaps another fifty to a hundred Nobles?" He shrugged. "The Vauphan army is larger, but we have more terrain to cross to get them here. Another two thousand are expected next week, and after that, it may be a while before more arrive. Our eastern border with Fiore is... tentative right now. The Giulea River Valley has always been contested lands between our nations. Right now, we're ceding territory to them." He sighed heavily. "Some in my lands are very upset about that. They want us to strike at Elista now, and retake the lands they've claimed, then build forts to hold them, so we can regroup to the east and retake Giulea once more."

Things sounded complicated for the prince. I felt for him. He was in an impossible situation. He had to defend and maintain his lands, but with Elista pushing, that meant losing lands in the east.

"Are the Fey truly that powerful?" Maverick asked.

Alvere smiled. "They are one of our best kept secrets. Though, in truth, they are not of Vauphan at all. Yet, they have decided we are their allies, and we've tried to maintain that relationship. We had a brief war with them when we tried to move north and settle the forests and hills there. It didn't go well for us, even though we probably outnumbered the Fey ten to one. We quickly ceded the lands back to them and apologized, trying to make them allies. That was over two hundred years ago. It took some time, but they have become... friends of Vauphan."

It was only then I recalled all the features the prince shared with Midnight... who was half-Fey.

"Are you—" I blurted before stopping myself.

Alvere smiled and sighed. "It seems my secret is out," he said softly. "I am half-Fey, yes. My Mother was Fey. I've... never met her. She may even be among those fighting with us, but I wouldn't know, even if I saw her." He seemed a bit sad, and I couldn't blame him. To have never known his mother... Though my birth mother had died when I was very young. I only had fleeting memories of her.

Maverick cleared his throat. "Ah... yes, we suspected as much," he said with a sidelong glance at me. "We have a mutual friend who is also half-Fey and the resemblance to you is... fascinating."

"I said nothing to them," Fin said, hands up in defense.

"But you are all keen of eye and quick of intellect. I can see that now." Alvere sighed. "I hope I can trust you all with this secret. Not even my own people know. Only my family knew, my mother and father, and they're both gone now."

"We will tell no one." Maverick eyed everyone just to make sure the message was clear.

I nodded.

Maverick sighed in the way he had a habit of doing, like the world itself was weighing upon his shoulders. "So," he said slowly, summing up. "Currently the tides favor Vauphan, six thousand to five thousand regular army, with your Fey versus our True-Bonded."

Alvere nodded.

"Cavalry?" Maverick asked.

Alvere nodded more, sitting forward. "As you know, Elista has never favored cavalry. From what we can tell, the Panthers have about five-hundred light cavalry; more like mobile infantry." Maverick nodded to that. "Vauphan has found a good use for Cavalry, though it is hard to outfit and train them. We have a thousand heavy cavalry."

"That's another thing in your favor then," Maverick said. Those armored horses could trample five times their numbers. We could win this battle tomorrow, if we wanted."

Alvere gave a grim smile. "As has been our thought as well, the trouble is... we cannot be certain of our losses. Which means we'd be a diminished force, trying to fortify when the larger numbers of Elistans arrived fresh. There are just too many unknowns."

"What about those ships that sailed for Elista to save you?" Maverick asked. "You sent that army north, didn't you? If so, I would have thought you'd have more men here?"

Alvere sighed. "Some of them returned to the capital and some, roughly five hundred, are here, supporting our forces, but most are still out on ships patrolling our coast. We can't risk an invasion by sea across Dyren's Bay. If the Elistans managed to get a force on land behind us..."

Maverick nodded understanding. "Too bad, we could use those men here." He seemed to mull things over for a moment before nodding to himself. "Let's see if we can't clarify a few things for you," Maverick said. "Legs, Amber, tomorrow you're scouting. Get as deep as you can into the Elistan camp, find out who's there and what's going on. Are they preparing for an offensive or digging in to defend? My guess would be the latter, but let's get some solid information for the prince."

"That would be appreciated, thank you," Alvere said. "I will have some dinner brought, then we can all rest, yes?"

With nods all around, it was decided.

We ate in silence for the most part. Alvere and Maverick stayed up to talk, but with a potentially long day ahead of me, I wanted to get to bed early.

The next day I was up early and found that Alvere wasn't in bed with me. When I went out into the common area of his pavilion he was sleeping on a long divan. The others weren't awake yet, so I sat next to him and shook him softly to wake him.

He smiled drowsily up at me. "Legs?"

"You didn't come to bed last night," I said, concerned.

"We hadn't had a chance to talk. We left things a bit... uncertain last time and I didn't want to presume, even though you chose my room."

What a gentleman.

I leaned down and kissed his forehead. "Then let's talk —" Though at that exact moment Maverick came out from his room. "—later before we sleep separately again, yes?"

He smiled, an eager liveliness coming to him as he seemed to realize what I was saying. "Yes," he breathed.

The others were up quickly and we all shared a warm breakfast before Amber and I were off to scout.

CHAPTER 18

AMBER COULDN'T CARRY ME AS A SPIDER; HER BUTTERFLY FORM wasn't strong enough. That meant I was walking... or flying. I made sure I had all my weapons, even some light armor: a breastplate with grieves and bracers, then I walked out of the Vauphani camp to the north, into the forest. I moved carefully through the woods until I was close to where the Elistans might have scouts, north and east of their camp.

Finding the tallest tree I could, I climbed it, first as a human, then getting to the very top as a spider. I spun a sort-of sail from my webbing and caught a south-westerly breeze, which carried me right over the Elistan camp.

I set down lightly on the pinnacle of a tent, then scurried down and moved carefully around the camp. After a morning of looking, I still hadn't found a command tent, but I kept heading deeper into the camp and hoped. Finally, I found a large tent which looked promising and scurried under the canvas. Inside were a group of men around a large table.

Jackpot, a command meeting.

I got a little closer, hiding behind one of the support beams for the large tent, then let my hairs do the listening.

"They could easily overrun us," one man said. I recognized the voice, but I wasn't sure from where. Perhaps my spider-sense-hearing was distorting it a little? That wasn't important, so I kept listening. The same man continued, saying, "Why do they wait?"

Another man, with a much deeper and more commanding voice answered. "Our spies report that they are expecting another four thousand men in the next ten days or so."

"But why wait?" the first man asked. "We'll have received some reinforcement by that time as well and—"

"Shut up and let me finish, Lynx!" The second man cut off the first.

Lynx?

A shudder ran through me. Lynx was the True-Bonded name of my first love, Kelen. I felt both startled and relieved. I hadn't expected him to be here, a commander at the front, but then... he'd been Chosen three years before me, four years ago now. He could have risen in the ranks of Panther House in that time. If he was here, perhaps I could talk to him, perhaps he'd listen to reason. I had to hope.

That reminded me, Cougar would probably be reaching the front lines soon. I hoped he'd heeded my warning and listened to what I'd said. I didn't know if his queries and doubts would help shed any truth on what was going on, but it might.

I listened in again, having missed a bit of what the more commanding voice had said. "...may overrun us, yes, but after the four thousand soon to come, they aren't expecting any more reinforcements for some time. Weeks away at best.

And, in that time, if their spies are as good as ours, they'd know we're expecting a significant force as well. It's all in the math."

The same man put on a lecturing tone. "Let's say they wait until the four thousand new troops arrive. Their ten thousand against our seven thousand — since the Pterolycus troops will be here by then — would probably mean a victory, but at what cost? Let's say they lose two thousand men and we lose the same. That means when the remaining troops from Pterolycus, along with the reserves from the capital arrive, we'll have ten thousand men, half of whom are fresh. They'll have eight thousand, all of whom are weary from the first battle and a desperate attempt to build fortifications. We'd wipe them out, send them running. So, it's a stalemate for now. Though it may not seem it, the advantage lays with us. We have fortifications in place, not much, but enough to slow their advance and cause them some pain in their first strike. And the longer we wait, the more troops we'll have. We can sit behind our growing fortifications and wait for them, perhaps even raid their camp to demoralize them. We've already won this fight, it's just a matter of how. Unless they get some miraculous addition to their forces, they cannot win here."

Silence hung in the room for a moment.

"And..." I couldn't see the man, but with how he said that single word, I felt like he was smiling, pompous, arrogant. "Though I haven't received the latest command updates, last I heard, we were going to ask Pegasus' troops to head south to a fleet of ships being readied." The man laughed. "With all the Vauphani troops being funneled north, their southern coast will be ripe for the taking. We can't keep those lands, of course, but we can pillage and burn their coast with impunity while their forces mass in the north. That will show them who's superior, show them that it's our right to hold these lands."

A cheer went up, but I'd heard enough. I needed to leave before I was sick. It was clear now who the true warmongers were among these two sides. This show of aggression by my own people — or those I'd thought were my own people — nauseated me.

I forced myself to wait, to see if there was any other information I might glean here, but the meeting broke up after that.

I quickly crawled outside and waited where I could see the exit. I caught sight of Lynx and followed him as he went to a modest sized tent and entered.

I crept under the canvas again and found a two-part pavilion, like Alvere's, but with only one room in the back and a much smaller sitting area in the front.

Lynx was alone, facing away from me, so I transformed and cleared my throat.

He turned and was so surprised he fell on his ass. I must have been quite a sight, an armored warrior woman with spear in hand.

"Hello, lover," I said, hoping that might defuse the tension. "Remember me?"

"Sara?" he breathed.

"It's Legs now. House Maverick."

He blinked and got up slowly. "You're…" He gave me the usual once-over that most men do, but then did it again, slower, truly taking me in. "You've changed."

"I like to think so."

He didn't approach or try to embrace me, which I'd thought one of his possible reactions. Instead, I caught a quick glance toward the room at the back of the tent. "I... you shouldn't be here. How did you get here? When did you get here?"

I followed his gaze, purposefully looking at the separator between the two rooms. "You're not alone?"

"Ah..."

"No, he's not," came a voice from the back area. A moment later a woman appeared. She wore only boots and a loose robe, casually wrapped around her. She and I looked at each other for a long moment before she gave a breathy laugh and dismissed me. And I could see why. She was everything I was, but... more. My height but with far more curves, especially at her bust, the lazily applied robe showing an abundance of cleavage. Yet the belt tying the garment closed showed a slender waist. Her hair was a shade off of mine, brown and wavy, but tinged with golden-red. And her eyes were a brilliant gold.

"Aren't you going to introduce us?" She asked, languidly, going to Lynx and draping herself over him, pressing close while looking at me the entire time.

He hesitated before saying: "Lady Claw, meet Lady Legs."

As everyone did, she looked at my legs, then she shrugged. From what I could see of hers — and it was a lot — she had me beat there too. "Pleasure to meet you," she purred. Then turned to Lynx and licked his lips before giving him a wet, messy kiss.

It was a show, for me. We all knew it. She pressed herself against him and whispered, "I'm going to have a bath and return to my tent. You're welcome to join me, if this doesn't take long." With that she pulled away from him and slinked over to me.

With a sour look, she ducked a little to give me a good

long sniff. Her lips pulled back, showing me her teeth as she hissed, "Hands off. He's mine." Then she veered into a small hunting cat with tan fur, roughly as large as a medium-sized dog and trotted out of the tent.

She'd done everything but pee on him to mark her territory.

I raised a brow. "She's... something."

"Sorry about that," Lynx said with a shrug. "She's a little possessive."

You don't say?

He sighed. "Why are you here, Legs?" He said it in an exasperated way. I had the feeling I'd gotten him in trouble with his lover and he knew he'd be paying for it later.

"I'm here about the war," I said, voice hushed. I didn't want anyone to overhear us.

It was his turn to raise a brow. "Maverick is sending us troops now? You're a long way from home. Why is Maverick House so concerned with what's happening up here?"

I grew grim. "Lynx, *everyone* should be concerned with what's happening 'up here,'" I said. "This isn't right. It needs to stop, and I was hoping I could talk to... an old friend who might have some pull here."

He scoffed. "Then you're in the wrong place. I have as much pull as a... mouse pulling a hay wagon. If you could hear the way Lord War was just putting me in my place, you'd know that."

"Lord War?" I said, curious. I'd assumed the other man talking in the meeting had been the leader of Panther House, Lord Jaguar. I had to wrack my memory for this new name.

"Oh yes. He's up from the capital. A *representative* of the Royal House here to *oversee* things." The way he said those two words made it clear the man wasn't overseeing so much as commanding. "Lord Jaguar is furious that he's not the one in control, but it seems there is more going on here than even we are privy to." He sighed heavily, shaking his head as he sought a chair and slumped into it.

I recalled the name now. It had been the mention of the Royal House. Lord War was the Field Marshal of the entire army of Elista, the highest-ranking officer. It was said he was a mean and vicious man who couldn't abide the ongoing peace Elista had with its neighbors. His presence here made perfect sense.

"We were doing well enough on our own the last three years," Lynx said. "Then he showed up and took control. I think he means to fully invade Vauphan. That's just crazy... isn't it?"

"Yes, it is." My tone was sour. But something else he'd said was curious. "You said something about 'the last three years'? That's how long you've been here?" I'd heard as much from Alvere, but wanted to hear confirmation from an Elistan source.

Lynx looked up at me blinking. "Yeah, doesn't everyone know how long we've been up here?"

"No, Lynx, *no one* knows. This war has been kept secret."

"Well... Maverick is in the South, so—"

"I was in Miraline just last year and I'd not heard anything about this." Miraline being the largest city in the North of Elista, and only three days or so from the boarder with Vauphan.

He cocked his head to one side. "Truly?"

It seems those here are doing a good job at keeping their own troops misinformed. Everyone here thinks the nation knows and those back home only found out recently as it's slowly coming out. This is... I can't fathom the work needed to keep all of this so... contained. Auwei seemed shocked and baffled.

I had to agree.

"No one knows what's going on here, Lynx." This was my chance. I sat myself in a chair next to Lynx, speaking quickly, whispering, hoping to get through to him. "This war, this invasion, whatever it is, it was kept a secret from the rest of the nation. No one knew. I don't know how that's possible, but someone on our side wanted to claim these lands in secret. It's the entire reason the Vauphani army is sitting out there. They have no clue why we took their lands and think we want more. Do we want more?" I asked, curious if he knew.

He shrugged. "I don't know. I'm still only a low-level Noble in Panther House. But I have a good head for tactics so I came here right after I was chosen for Panther." He too spoke quietly, perhaps a bit caught up in my tale of secrecy. "We were told Vauphan was planning an invasion." His volume dropped even more. "Not just of Elista, but... that they wanted to claim the Mists!"

That shocked me. "Truly?"

Oh, that's interesting indeed. That rumor would certainly worry many Nobles. I got the sense Auwei had hit on something, but if so, she wasn't sharing it yet.

"Yes. We were told their provinces near the border were crawling with spies and scouts and a large force was on its way, though it would take time for it to get here, and that the only way to confirm we held the Mists was to take the northern Vauphani provinces first, before they were swarming with troops. So... we did."

I blinked. I knew that wasn't true, but I couldn't say anything or I'd give away that I knew more about Vauphan than I should. But still the question remained... why? Why would Elista spin such a tale of impending invasion to prompt our own counter-invasion? I didn't think Lynx would know, but I had to ask.

"Why, Lynx?" I whispered. "It must be clear to you now, since it took the Vauphani army some time to get here, that that story was... just a story. So why would we want to invade their lands?"

He shook his head, and when he spoke his voice was hard to hear. It was clear he was afraid of speaking about this. "I don't know, and I don't want to ask. The ones who question things... Legs, they've disappeared."

"Nobles?" I said feeling a realization coming on.

Oh... do you think? Auwei asked.

Yes, I do.

"Yes! And some high-ranking ones."

I swallowed hard. I was willing to bet they hadn't disappeared. I was near-to-certain they were dead, and not just dead, but with their Lumani killed as well. That old rumor came back to me. Nobles and their Lumani dying. Before, I didn't know why, but I think I did now. Anyone who got too close to this massive secret — anyone who threatened it — died. And their Lumani were killed to keep the secret from passing on to their next host.

That's... I can't... Gah! I felt Auwei's anger as my own.

"Spirits!" I whispered and rose suddenly. "I have to go."

Lynx rose, looking a bit shaken by his own words. He seemed concerned for me. "If... what you're thinking is what I'm thinking and you're going to tell someone about all this... Legs, they'll disappear you too." He came close, hands on my shoulders. "Just... be careful."

I smiled. "I will. Don't worry." I stepped back and turned away. Then turned back. I didn't want to shock him when I didn't leave the normal way. I smiled. "Now, if you don't mind, I'll go out the way I came in." I winked at him then veered into my spider form. He started, then laughed.

"Ah... farewell, Legs."

I crawled out from the canvas and began the very long walk back to the Vauphani camp. I had more than a few interesting things to report.

CHAPTER 19

I DIDN'T WANT TO RISK ANYONE MISTAKING ME FOR AN ENEMY, so I remained in spider form as I crossed back across the barren would-be battlefield to the Vauphan camp. I didn't return to myself until I was safely within Alvere's pavilion, which meant it was well after dark by the time I finally reached it.

I returned to myself and immediately slumped into one of the camp chairs. Amber, Jack, and Maverick must have been in bed, but Fin and Alvere were still up, chatting quietly. They both looked at me, stunned. Then Fin rose, putting a meaty hand on Alvere's shoulder.

"Good night, friend," he said and made his way to his room.

Alvere came to me, kneeling beside the chair. "How...?" He shook his head. "No, your report can wait for tomorrow, you look exhausted. What can I do?"

"A bath would be lovely," I said, feeling filthy after crawling through mud all day.

"And... after that?" He asked, voice hushed. There were others around.

"After that, you're taking me to bed," I said, voice husky partly from fatigue and partly with anticipation. "We can have that talk I promised while I bathe... while *you* bathe me." I grinned at him.

Alvere smiled so wide he looked a bit silly. He nodded, saying: "Most of the men and women in the army bathe in the river. It's mountain run-off, so it's cold all year and they don't stay long in those waters. I think I can get you something better. Wait here." He rose and left the pavilion.

I must have dozed. Alvere woke me with a soft touch to my shoulder. His kind beryl-blue eyes and sympathetic smile were exactly what I wanted to see waking up.

"I'm having a tub brought in and some hot water. It may take a bit of time. Rest for now." He leaned down and kissed my cheek, and I smiled, eyes drooping shut.

I woke again several times as servants came and went bringing and filling the tub.

Then Alvere woke me. "It's ready," he said, pointing to the large, roughly oval shaped metal tub. He helped me up, then scooped me into his arms — he was stronger than he looked — and carried me the few steps to the basin, setting me down next to it.

I was so tired, I stood there for a long moment staring at the water trying to remember what the next step was. I tried to step in, but Alvere stopped me.

"You're still dressed."

Yup, I was. "Fix that, please," I said with a weary grin.

He didn't need to be told twice and began removing my armor and clothes. The arousal and heat filling my body as his slender fingers brushed my flesh woke me further. After that, I made it easier for him, helping where I could, until I stood naked before him.

Those jewel-toned pools of eyes devoured me.

I couldn't get enough of him looking at me like that.

"Not right now," I said with a soft smile and a shake of my head. "I'm dirty."

He quirked a half-grin, raising one brow, then motioned to the tub. "You wanted to... talk?"

I stepped in gingerly, finding the water warm, but not hot. It must be hard to get the water warmed significantly. Still, I slid down, knees up, until I was reclining in the waters. It was wonderful.

"Yeah," I drew the word out. "Talk." And I knew I should, before these warm waters lulled me to sleep again.

"You... wanted me to bathe you?" he asked.

"Yup, please do."

"So, your... complications have... gone away?" He reached for some soap and a sponge.

"Yup." I needed to get this all out now. Hopefully I was awake enough to do it properly.

Alvere began to bathe me. His hands worked with soap and sponge to lather me up and scrub me all over. It felt delightful, sensuous and caring.

So, how to say this...? Silence and Sparrow were on board. They knew of the prince and I very much wanted to let him in, fully.

"The complications are gone," I began softly. I felt weightless, floating in a warm sea, which pleasantly washed over me. The words came with a sort of slow and sleepy, dream-like quality. "I am promised to know one, *but* there are others I love... Silence and Sparrow. I do not wish to limit myself to one lover. But... that means everyone I'm with needs to know how I feel, needs to know there are others I love and will be with." I smiled then as he paused in his ministrations, his gaze caught on mine. "I love you all, but when I am with you, I am with only you. There are no others on my mind. You are fully mine, and I am fully yours. If... if you are well with this, then I—"

His kiss stopped my words, impassioned and hard, soft lips pressing with a raging desire held in check for too long. Yet he pulled away quickly to say, "I am well with it." Then his lips were on mine again, his sponge forgotten as his hands dipped into the waters to roam my skin.

I came up for breath a moment later, loving how his hands knew exactly where to reach, how hard to touch, how to move and press. I moaned softly, but then said, "I'm still filthy. Give me a moment?"

He withdrew, hunger in those intense jewel-blue eyes.

I dunked my head under the water, finding the soap and scrubbing at my face and hair for a moment — coming up for air as needed — to cleanse myself.

When I came up for the last time, he had a towel ready. I accepted it as I stood, drying myself, and he watched with rapt focus, which made me blush.

I stepped out of the bath to dry my legs, and as soon as I was done, he scooped me up again and carried me to his bed. He placed me atop the fur-lined covers as he quickly stripped from his clothes. I gave a little gasp as he freed his erection and it leaped up to stand proud before him, thick and red and ready. I snuggled under the sheets and when he joined me, I put a finger to his lips.

"Please remember there are others close by and it's late," I whispered. "Let's try not to wake them." And with those words my fantasy from the library at Hedgewild returned, flashing in my mind. We were hot and needful, standing with me pressed to a bookshelf as we took our desire from each other with heated gasps, trying to remain quiet... just in case.

If I hadn't been aroused before, that steamy memory made sure I was now.

He nodded and when I removed my finger, his lips sought mine, desperate and needful. We pressed close, skin to skin, and I felt the rigid length of his shaft pressing against me. Between the sensuous bathing and my torrid fantasy, I was wet and ready for him, but he was in no hurry to enter me. His fingers found my folds first, pressing and playing, arousing me further. I opened my legs, inviting him in, but instead, when he shifted next, moving on top of me, it was to kiss his way down my body. He pressed his lips to my neck, then the soft curves of my breast and the hardened buds of my nipples. We both let out soft moans of pleasure as he worked upon those sensitive mounds for a prolonged moment, his hand hard upon my ever-more-slick folds.

Then... he kissed down my belly, disappearing under the sheets, bringing his lips to my ready entrance. He pressed the flat of his tongue against me, moving it slowly over the area, before flicking the tip across my clit in an amazing shock of pleasure. My hands dug through his hair, pressing him close, as his lips found me again, sucking and nibbling, his tongue darting inside me.

Sparrow's ministrations with her lips had been soft and tentative, slow to build and producing a gradual tidal wave of bliss. Alvere was intense and rough, hard and needful, and my ecstasy quickly overwhelmed me.

I reached a peak and gasped as my body stiffened and shuddered, back arching. My hands left his hair to grab my own breasts, pressing and tweaking my nipples to enhance my pleasure.

And just as I waned from that peak, Alvere stopped with his lips and moved up. I felt the press of his erection against me as his head and shoulders emerged from under the covers, gaze intent on mine... as if asking permission.

I nodded, wordless, and he smiled. He entered me slowly, watching my lip-biting reaction. He was thicker than Silence, and I could feel every inch of his hard flesh against all manner of wonderful places, filling me. His loins pressed to mine, grinding down hard. Spirits! He felt so big within me, even though he hadn't seemed that much larger than Silence.

His body trembled, and his eyes rolled up then closed for a moment as he pressed hard within and against me. He swallowed and his eyes opened, gaze meeting mine.

"You're too much for me," he whispered. "I don't know how long I can—"

I reached up, drawing his face down to mine, loving the feel of his body on mine, the press of his solid planes against my soft hills. I tasted myself upon his lips as we kissed and still drew him closer, deeper.

I pushed him back a moment to say, "I'm tired, Alvere, and you've already given me pleasure. Take yours."

That was all he needed. He gasp-grunted with each short, hard thrust, pressing his body to mine in amazing ways. The grinding of his pubic bone against my clit had me moaning and gasping as well soon after. He swelled within me as his pace grew frenzied. He was close. I too felt another orgasm building, ready to release.

With a final thrust and a quiet grunt, a full-body shudder took him and he exploded within me.

I was so close to my own release. I just needed him in the right place. So, I reached down to grab his buttocks, pulling him to me, pressing him where I needed him. He twitched and pressed closer, shifting over me, which made my bliss rise higher, but the release still eluded me.

"Oh, gods!" he whispered, "I can't... you're so..." Then another shudder took him as his release pulsed again and again, hot inside me.

"I just need—"

"I know," he whispered. One of his hands slid down between us, finding my clit. With a twitch of his fingers I felt a white-hot flash of ecstasy and bliss surged through me.

I bit my lip to keep from crying out. My sheath contracted, gripping his erection tight, squeezing. He gave a jaw-dropping, wide-eyed, silent shout as his release seemed to culminate into a single moment of ultimate bliss. His body tensed above me, he jerked and shifted for a long moment before he finally fell onto me, spent.

I was right there with him through that extended climax, feeling his pounding heart through his shaft inside me, matching my own as I shuddered and tensed with my own world-melting joy.

Then we lay, gasping and panting together for a long moment.

"I've never..." he whispered. "No woman... That was incredible." His head next to mine warmed my ear with his breathy praise. He nibbled my ear, sliding his tongue lightly along the ridges and hollows.

That sent a new thrill through me as I said, "For me too. I've never felt anything like that." It was the truth. Silence had always been intense and immediate; a spike of pleasure that I was quite happy with. But this had been a ridge-line of passion, rising higher and higher before it had finally, blessedly all come crashing down.

Alvere withdrew and slumped to one side of me. One of his arms remained over me, warm and comforting.

I floated in that strange place between wake and sleep when I heard his words, as if from a distance. "I may be required to marry and I may be with other women, but I don't think any of them will ever compare to you, Legs. I love you." I felt his soft kiss on my shoulder.

That warmed me as I sank into the depths of sleep... and my dreams of him and me... and Silence and Sparrow, warmed me even further still. I slept *very well* that night.

The next morning, once everyone was up, I gave my report, feeling an odd mix of elation and confused dismay. I longed to be in Alvere's arms again, feel him on me and in me and... ohhhhh! But I also had to keep to my duties and that meant telling everyone of what I'd found out from Lynx the previous day.

"They told him that Vauphan wanted the Mists?" Alvere asked, clearly confused. He sighed, raising a brow. "We've always been curious about that magical land, but haven't had any great desire to have it. Honestly, I think most of us believed it would somehow defend itself, or the Lumani would, keeping us from claiming it if we tried." He shrugged.

"I think your theory about why the Nobles and Lumani are being killed is a good one," Maverick said to me. "It makes a sick sort of sense." He shook his head. "And I think it's safe to assume Lord War is a part of the conspiracy. Which makes it more and more likely that the Royal House is behind all of this."

I couldn't believe the queen would do this, but I had to agree. With Hale and War both being a part of what was going on... the Royals were certainly heavily involved.

Amber reported on the state of their fortifications. Trenches and earthworks with palisades were going up on the far side of the battle-field, and were nearly complete. They spanned perhaps five miles, from the edge of the forest to the north, to the rushing waters of the Sacha River in the south. Yet it was only a front at the moment. A force would be able to easily skirt through the forest to go around it, or brave the frigid river waters on the other side. She also reported that the majority of the Panther Nobles she knew were already here, even a few from Pterolycus.

"They're not preparing for an advancement, not yet," she said, smooth alto voice like silk as she spoke. "From Legs' report, it sounds like they mean to hold here, at least until Vauphan cedes these lands and their army leaves."

"Though," Alvere said with bitter disgust. "As soon as we do, I fear they'll claim more. Their attacks in the south are just a feint, but we'll have to draw troops from somewhere to defend, in addition to constant patrols by our navy. And if we take troops from this front, I do not trust them to remain behind their walls."

No one countered that statement. We all knew it could very well be true.

Alvere sat forward, head in hands. "No matter my choice, my people die." His voice was heavy with sorrow. "What do I do?"

To that, none of us had an answer.

CHAPTER 20

SILENCE

SILENCE WAS RELIEVED WHEN HEDGEWILD FINALLY CAME INTO sight as the day dawned.

Sparrow's dire news had gotten those from House Maverick in the capital moving quickly. They'd been away from the capital that day, heading south. And they hadn't stopped, traveling night and day, taking turns driving the cart Midnight had acquired. In Grovner's Green, they'd halted long enough to warn the small village that an army might soon be marching through. And when they'd left, Midnight and Sparrow had flown ahead to the manor, to get the others starting the preparations to leave.

By the time Silence and Foggy arrived, the house was in an uproar as everyone gathered their own things, along with items belonging to those who weren't present that they thought might be required or sentimental.

For those who'd been here the longest, it wasn't an easy process.

Silence didn't have a lot and gathered his things quickly. With that done, Ant ordered him up to the observatory to help Crane.

When he arrived, he found the usually staid and proper woman tearfully muttering to herself as she threw handfuls of paper into the roaring hearth fire behind Maverick's desk.

She looked up and gave him a sad smile. She'd always been so removed and emotionless. Her voice was trembling when she said, "How much can you carry?" Then shook her head. "No, I need Ant." She had several trunks out, packed with the books from the shelves to either side of the hearth. "We need to save as much of our history as we can."

"I'm stronger than I look," Silence said and, closing one of the trunks — which only just latched shut, stuffed as it was — he lifted it easily. "Everyone discounts a mouse," he said as he carried the chest toward the stairs. "But they can lift their own bodyweight easily. I'll be back for the rest in a moment." Mice also had exceptional balance and speed, so Silence was able to hurry down the many stairs from the tower to the front of the manor. He loaded the chest onto the wagon — which was quickly filling up and another was being brought around — before hurrying back up to get another chest.

The army wouldn't be here tomorrow or even the next day. The capital was a two-day ride in a carriage, and armies did not move that quickly. But still, everyone wanted to be away with all haste. Advanced scouts on fast horses — or True-Bonded with bird forms — could be here soon enough. So, the two wagons, loaded past capacity, were rolling out just before noon. Tusk drove one, with Princess beside her. A stone-faced Crane, matched with Midnight, led the other. Sparrow and Dove circled high above us as their avatars, keeping an eye out for trouble. Foggy, Fennec,

Ant, and Silence himself, walked beside the slow-moving wagons.

It only occurred to Silence now to ask: "Where are we going?"

Ant answered. "Fin's family are fishermen from a small village not too far south of here, down the coast a little. He bought a cottage there a while ago, and Maverick liked the idea of a second home, a place where anyone could go for some privacy so he helped to ah... refurbish it."

A single cottage? How big was it? "Will we all fit?" Silence asked, looking at the group and the two wagons piled with chests and sacks.

Ant gave a low chuckle. "Maverick did a lot of... refurbishing."

Silence didn't know what that meant, but he supposed he'd find out soon enough.

They reached the Sea Road — one of the few true stone roads in the south, which ran the entire length of the southern shores — and turned south. By late afternoon, the seaside cliffs began to slope down, and Silence saw a village up ahead.

Surprisingly, they didn't go there. Even before they got to the village a small cottage at the side of the road came into view. And that's where they stopped.

Ant knocked on the door instead of just entering. Silence was curious who lived here, if the cottage belonged to Fin. A spry man in his later years with a wiry body, large eyes, and mostly grey hair answered. He looked around quickly then nodded.

"Silence, meet Clam. He's the one who did the refurbishments on the cottage, so as a reward we let him live here." The way Ant kept saying "refurbishment" gave Silence the impression it was far more than just new thatching on the roof. Also, this cottage looked large enough for a small family, no more. If Clam lived here... where were the rest of them going to fit?

"You all unload, I'll get the home-fires burning!" Clam said with a grin missing several teeth, before ducking back inside. Silence helped to unload the wagons, though when he went inside the old man was nowhere to be seen in the one-room house. Odd.

When the wagons were unloaded Fennec and Foggy drove them away, toward the village.

"They'll sell the wagons to a teamster," Ant said in response to Silence's curious look. "We'll probably be here for a while, and hopefully Fin will have returned by the time this is all over and can help with transporting things back to Hedgewild." Ant smiled reassuringly. "This will all be resolved soon enough, you'll see." He put a thick hand on Silence's shoulder and led him inside.

Silence decided to ignore the contradiction of: *we'll probably be here for a while* and *this will all be resolved soon*. Ant was trying to make him feel better, but he doubted anything could truly allay his concerns in that moment.

It was cramped inside with all the people and the cargo from the wagons. One end of the house was a living and sleeping area with a bed and a few comfortable looking chairs. There was a hearth at that end, already warm. The other side was a kitchen area with a long table, shelves well stocked with all manner of provisions and another hearth for cooking. And still no sign of Clam.

Crane went to the far end on the bedroom side and slid her finger into a knothole in the wall, silently pulling open a hidden door. Princess and Tusk moved the two chairs out of the way, onto the bed, making a cleared area to move things to the door... and beyond.

Eager and curious, Silence picked up a small chest and carried it to the door behind Ant. The space beyond the door was narrow, perhaps two feet wide? Since it was the corner of the house there was a small landing, then stairs descended steeply down to the right, into darkness. Ant went slowly, having to move sideways because of his bulk, the chest he was carrying now lengthwise under one arm.

Silence was skinny, but even so, he and the chest he was carrying could — just barely — fit if he walked sideways as well.

Several steep steps led down to another small landing. The outer wall of the cabin, beside Silence, transitioned from wood, to fieldstone foundation, to solid stone carved smooth. Then came another right-hand turn with a low ceiling here, probably the floor of the house above as they moved underneath it. Ant had to duck awkwardly, but Silence made it under with only a bit of a nod of his head. After that, the stairs weren't quite as steep and the stone-carved hall broadened. After about a dozen steps, they made another right turn. Another set of stairs descended for a long stretch. Small torches on the walls barely lit the long downward hall. They came to a landing and a switchback, then down more stairs to an open area... a cave, but with the walls carved smooth and straight.

"Silence! You're holding things up!" Princess said behind him. He hadn't realized he'd stopped to gawk and moved to one side, setting the chest down. Then he truly took in the large room. It was roughly as wide as the length of the house above, with heavy carpets covering most of the smooth stone floor. There were two hearths, on either side of the room. Silence tried to re-imagine things in his head and could see how the chimneys for these hearths might go up right under the hearths in the house's bedroom and kitchen.

The smoke from those chimneys would seem to be coming from the house... ingenious! Yet the room was long and spacious. There was a sitting area before the hearth on one side, and a kitchen with a long table with benches, probably able to sit ten to a side, close to the other hearth. On the far side were a number of tunnel-like windows, with long shafts through the stone between the glass on this side and the edge of the cliff on the far side. They would let in some light, but only have direct sun first thing in the morning when the sun was close to the horizon.

"The bedrooms are down here," Ant said. He pointed to another set of stairs heading down, back behind Silence. Leaving off with the lugging of supplies for the moment, Silence followed Ant down, deeper into the stone of the cliffs. Another long set of stairs led down to a landing, then a switchback and more stairs down. At the bottom was a hallway, perpendicular to the stairway. Smooth stone archways — hung with heavy cloth curtains instead of doors — dotted one side of the hall at even intervals.

Silence peeked past the curtains into the closest room. It contained a bed and a small chest next to it, which could double as a nightstand. That was it. There was a window, like the ones up above, glass on this end of a long tunnel out.

"How...?" Silence whispered. This place was amazing, and someone had painstakingly carved these perfect tunnels and rooms. "Who...?" but then he remembered who. He turned to Ant. "Clam did all of this?"

Ant nodded. "Bet you didn't know clams were good at digging through stone."

"I didn't, no." He looked down the long hall. There had to be at least twenty doors. "Still, this must have taken him his entire life."

"Only about seven years, actually."

Silence marveled at that, shaking his head.

"It's not the most comfortable place. It can get very cool down here, but the beds have lots of covers and we have lots of wood for the hearths upstairs." Ant rested a strong hand on Silence's slender shoulder. "Come on, let's help the others unload."

Silence nodded and followed Ant up the many stairs once more.

Seven years to make all of this... Amazing!

Clam had prepared a dinner for them in the main hall by the time they had everything unloaded down into the caverns. It was also about that time that Fennec and Foggy returned from the village, and Dove and Sparrow returned from keeping an eye on things above.

The news wasn't good.

"We got out just in time," Sparrow said with a note of sorrow in her voice. "Advanced scouts reached Hedgewild this evening. It will be crawling with men soon. She shuddered at that thought. Silence couldn't blame her.

They ate in silence that evening. They'd lost their home, Their true home. And these caves were beginning to feel more like a prison than a cozy hideaway.

Silence hoped that this madness would not continue much longer, but he could see no end in sight, and from the silence of the others... neither could they.

CHAPTER 21

WE WERE A SOMBER GROUP THAT DAY AS WE TRIED TO COME up with ideas to stop what Elista planned for Vauphan. But no resolutions were forthcoming. After supper, when Alvere asked me if I wished to walk in the woods, I accepted happily. We strolled, hand in hand, through the camp and then into the woods to the north.

The edge of the woods was mostly open, with large swaths of mostly flat ground and little underbrush between the sparsely placed trees. But very quickly, heading deeper, the trees grew closer together, and the bushes and brush thicker.

Yet Alvere moved with purpose and seemed to know a path. So, I followed, still holding his hand as we began the climb up a heavily forested hill.

I could feel his tension, the weight of the coming war upon him. He didn't want his men to die, and I believed he didn't want the mostly innocent men who'd be on the front lines for Elista to die either. It was all so senseless. He sighed repeatedly as we walked, then the forest suddenly gave way to a clearing at the top of the hill. A single tree stood at the peak of the knoll, tall with a wide tangle of sprawling branches and a thick trunk. Alvere took me straight to it.

When we drew close, I noticed something odd. Small, low branches, which seemed to have been carved flat on top, progressed up around the tree... like steps! We mounted those, circling tightly upward — we had to release hands for this part — until we came to a wide platform in the high branches of the tree. From the bottom, this had looked like a tangled web of branches, but from the top... they were perfectly smooth, a lattice of merged branches with only tiny holes between. The trunk continued up and there were branches above us, but this entire level was open and flat, all the way around the tree.

Oh, this is wonderful! Auwei said in awe.

I had to agree.

Alvere stood there, ignoring the wonder of this strange tree and instead looking out over the forest and the plains beyond. Admittedly, it was a spectacular sight, sun setting behind a bank of clouds, turning the sky turquoise and the clouds to yellow and orange flame.

I grasped his hand again and squeezed it. "Thank you for bringing me here, it's wonderous!"

He smiled faintly. "I found it not long after coming here. I felt... drawn to this place. I think it's a Fey lookout." Those beryl-blue eyes twinkled at me, but only for a moment before growing dark and dim, and he looked away. "What are we going to do Legs?" he asked, sounding a bit hopeless.

I didn't know and couldn't answer.

But perhaps I could take his mind off his troubles, even if only for a moment... just not here. It was a bit too exposed and open at the top of this tree. It was my turn to pull him. I tugged his arm and got him moving. We descended out from the branches and once back on solid ground, feeling less exposed, I turned to him and threw my arms around him for a surprise kiss.

His eyes widened. He was stunned only for a moment before I could feel some of his tension drain away as he held me.

I lingered in the kiss for some time, allowing it to develop organically until our mouths were wide: desperate and deep. Then I drew back with a mischievous grin. "I want to give you something," I said softly. "Help you forget about everything and think only of me, even if only for a time."

He smiled and raised a brow in question. I don't think he was expecting me to slip down to my knees and undo the tie on his breeches.

"Oh, Legs, no. Prince or King or whatever, you will never have to kneel before me. I—" he gasped as I ignored what he'd said and, pulling out his stiffening erection, ran the tip of my tongue along the underside of his shaft.

"Legs... Oh!"

My mouth enveloped him and I drew him deep, moving my hand down to his heavy sack and testing its weight in my palm. His length went rigid as I worked my tongue and teeth over him. His objections stopped, turning to shuddering, gasping breaths. When I stole a glance up at him, his head was tilted back, looking at the branches above us.

My intent was not to work him to release as I had with Silence. No, I wanted him hard and ready for the next bit.

I withdrew my lips but grasped him hard with my hand, squeezing a little. He looked down at me as I ran my tongue around his tip. "Are you thinking only of me now?" I asked playfully.

"Gods, yes!" he breathed.

"Good, because I want you concentrating fully on me for this next part." I rose and went to untie the belt of my skirt.

"Allow me," he breathed.

Curious, I moved my hands away, waiting for his touch... but instead he simply waved a hand and the belt undid itself and my skirt fell away. With another wave the tie at the bottom of my blouse — to keep it up over my belly-button, just in case — undid and the loose shirt lifted off.

I blinked.

He winked. "I'll tell you later," he said as he came for me hungrily, his erection throbbing from my previous minis-trations.

I always seemed to forget how strong those slender arms of his were. He lifted me easily, and I threw my arms around his neck, legs around his waist as he lowered me upon his solid flesh.

It was my turn to gasp at his sudden thrusting, but I quickly progressed from tight and pained to receptive and eager. He turned, pressing my back to the rough bark of the tree, but I didn't care. It was the price of sex in nature, rocks and bark and roughness.

Raised as I was upon him, his lips found my breasts, kissing around their fullness as he picked up his pace, hard and needful inside me.

With my hands behind his head, I hugged him to me, encouraging his work upon my bosom as I tilted my head back. "Yes, my love!" I urged him.

His release came quickly, as I had suspected it would. He kissed his way up my neck and I tilted my head down to kiss him as he tensed and throbbed and trembled through his orgasm.

He gave me a pained look. I hushed the apology I felt coming with another kiss to his lips, then the soft words, "This was for you."

Something shifted in his look then, his clear blue eyes

twinkling. He grinned. "Then the next will be for you... and I'm certain I'll remain distracted."

I smiled, liking the sound of that.

He withdrew and I was carefully set down. Then he removed his shirt and, with another wave of his hand, it wrapped itself around the rough bark of the tree. "Sorry if that hurt," he whispered. If it had, I hadn't noticed, though I'd probably have a scrape or two. He pulled me close and we kissed for a long moment again, as I felt his erection revivify between us.

When he released my lips, he turned me around slowly. I was a bit confused by this until I felt him pull me close again, his firm chest against my back. His arms around me seeking, stroking, caressing. He had much more ease of access in this position to touch me. His lips were soft upon my shoulders and neck, as I pulled my hair up and away for him. His one hand was firm upon my breasts as his other stroked softly over my folds. He had all the control, all the power, but I was the benefactor of everything. I leaned my head back upon his shoulder, looking up at the branches once more as his hands worked my arousal up to body-trembling heights.

I felt him shift and move. His erection slid between my legs then up to my opening. I was far more ready for him this time as his fingers, slick with my wetness, helped to guide him in. And though he could not go deep, this angle felt amazing!

I moaned and moved against him, letting him hear my appreciation. And he whispered in my ear: "I love you, Legs. I need you. You are my world."

Good, that was the point of this exercise. It was also pleasing to hear, and with his slow thrusting and miracle fingering, I merged those hot words into the whirlwind of passion swirling within me. He did not pick up his pace, but simply kept up all his precious teasing touches upon my now trembling flesh. For a moment his one hand left my loins to rise to my other breast and both hands grasped me hard, pressing me to him. I gasped and felt a mini-peak of bliss, body tensing. Then he moved those strong but agile fingers out to tease my hardened nipples and that peak rose and built.

"Yes," I gasped. "I'm so close!" I needed to let him know. If he was going to let loose, now was the time.

He tugged at an earlobe with his lips as his hands, hard-pressing, slid down my body to the front of my hips, one slipping a little lower still to press against the raging nub of my clit as he did indeed pick up his pace.

The first orgasm bucked me forward. I pressed my hips back against him, needing him deeper as I put my hands against the tree — now covered by his shirt — and used that as leverage to roll my hips back with each of his thrusts. I could hear his heavy breaths, but only barely over my own rough gasps as he slipped his fingers over my clit again and roused a second and more powerful wave of full-body bliss. I froze, tense and trembling as he thrusted harder still until his release. And feeling that heart-pounding surge inside me sent me spinning into an oblivion of ecstasy, my body going weak.

But his strong hands were there to guide me, help me up, as we trembled together for a long moment. Eventually he helped me to lay with my back upon him as he reclined on the ground. It was his turn for the rocks and roughness.

It was a long time before I could speak, asking, "What are you thinking about now?"

"You," he said kissing my shoulder. "And right now, I couldn't imagine thinking of anything else." His hips bucked with an after-shock of bliss as he gasped. Then I gasped. Then we laughed together. "I love you, Legs, thank you. You are the most amazing woman."

"You're pretty amazing yourself. Don't forget it. When you're troubled by anything else, just remember me and how amazing we are together and know you can do anything."

Awkwardly, we shifted so we could touch lips. The kiss was deep but brief.

"I will," he whispered. "I will."

We lay together for a while longer, as the evening grew dark, before finally separating and dressing.

"What was that thing you did, with my clothes and your shirt?" I asked, remembering now.

Oh yes, that was fascinating! I'm so curious! Auwei was near to giddy. This was what Lumani lived for, the many new and interesting experiences of this world.

He laughed. "I don't tend to show that to anyone, even my own people. It's a Fey thing."

I raised a brow. "Oh?"

"Yes, Fey magic comes through the working of material. Some are good with wood, others with metal, some with clay and earth, others with living beings, and some... with cloth." He flipped his hand and put his arms up and his shirt slid itself over him. He grinned.

I recalled how Midnight had made that branch appear then disappear from the wooden support in the barn, when interrogating that brute.

Oh yes, you're right; fascinating!

"It's actually very useful. I don't need armor, I can make my own clothes as hard as steel. It takes little concentration now, I've been practicing it most of my life. I can unravel threads, and make them reach across a room to get a cup or pour a kettle. Again, I don't do it often, only when I'm alone, and I'm sure I'm not nearly as proficient as a full Fey would be, but..." He shrugged. "It can come in handy from time to time."

I imagined so. "That is amazing," I said and meant it.

"I wouldn't say it's any more or less amazing than you becoming a spider or having powers of such an animal."

I nodded. "True."

I am pretty amazing, aren't I? Auwei said with mock modesty.

You are. I laughed inwardly with her.

Alvere and I chatted, comparing our powers as we made our way back down the hill and into the forest. Apparently, he also had exceptional night vision. While I had to trust to my spider-sense in the dark.

And perhaps it was because it was dark and I was already concentrating on my spider sense that I sensed something. I stopped us both with an outstretched arm and a quick, quiet, "Hush."

He looked at me inquiring as my hairs prickled and listened. There were people around... many people... creeping through the forest. It took me a moment longer to sense the number and direction. A force of perhaps five hundred, moving west to east through the forest.

I pulled Alvere close, hot breath on his ear in the barest of whispers. "It's an Elistan raid on your camp!"

I felt his body tense.

Neither of us had brought weapons.

We were trapped, behind the enemy, with no way to warn the Vauphan of the impending raid.

CHAPTER 22

We hid in some brush, huddled together as the night grew chill. The force in the woods was moving slowly and hadn't turned south toward the camp yet. I was confused by this, until I thought of something. I whispered my suspicions to Alvere, so close my lips brushed his ear as I breathed the words. "I think they're trying to get *behind* the camp."

He made a face. My night-sight wasn't as good as his, but I could still see him by the faint, few speckles of moonlight filtering down through the branches above. Shifting, he breathed in my ear and the hot breath and soft voice made me shiver just a little... even if it wasn't sweet-nothings he was whispering.

"Why? Five hundred men could do some damage if they surprised us, but... where will they retreat to when finished?"

I couldn't answer. But they must have some plan.

Luckily, if this troop passed us by, we'd be able to run back to camp and warn them, hopefully before the attack occurred.

So, as soon as I sensed that the five hundred were far enough away that it would be safe to move, we rose and began our dash for the edge of the woods.

But we only made it a few feet.

Once again, I stopped Alvere and we ducked into bushes. "More!" I whispered. Another group sneaked through the woods from the west. My spider sense had picked them up, and I could see distant shadows moving among the trees.

"How many?" Alvere whispered to me.

"Another five hundred is my guess," I breathed in return.

But these troops found spots to hide and hunkered down.

"An attack from all sides?" Alvere whispered to me.

I nodded, it seemed likely. We needed to warn the Vauphani camp.

You could float like you did to get into the Elistan camp, Auwei suggested.

Yeah, if the breeze is right. I sighed. It might be our only option. The trouble was, I wouldn't be able to bring Alvere with me, he'd be stuck here, alone, with enemies virtually all around him.

I didn't want to leave him, but someone had to warn the Vauphani. I put my lips to his ear once more, to fill him in. "If I get high enough in one of these trees, I can float on spider silk and probably fly over this group to warn your men, but... you can't come." I felt his hesitation. He wanted to turn his head and speak, but I continued. "You need to flee, go back to that tree or find some Fey, get to safety. I'll warn the camp."

I felt his jaw tense.

He drew in several deep breaths, before finally nodding.

Turning to me, he whispered, "Good luck, my love." Then he kissed my cheek.

"And to you, my love," I whispered. Then with a final kiss, we parted. He rose and padded away as silent as the night, back up the hill.

I veered to spider form and scampered up a tree to the very top. I did as I'd done before, weaving a sail of spider-silk and catching a breeze.

But the breeze was strong and from the east. It pushed me in the wrong direction until I caught on another tree.

There was another option though...

I scampered down the tree to a branch which would support me as a human, then transformed back.

I launched myself, with my powerful legs, up and angled out of the forest to the south. This worked, though I did tear through the upper branches of a few trees, acquiring a few scrapes and ripping my clothes.

Once I'd hit my apex and began to fall, I transformed back to a spider and quickly wove another small sail of silk, to slow me a bit before I landed. This way I wouldn't scare any of the Vauphani sentries, nor would I alert the Elistans in the woods.

I floated to the ground at the edge of the camp, then ran for all my little eight legs would carry me for Alvere's tent. Once I reached it, I returned to my form and called out for the others.

Only Maverick was still in the front part of the pavilion. "Attack! Surprise attack from all sides!" I hissed at him as I ran for my armor and weapons.

He was up in an instant and roused the others.

"I'll get help!" Fin said and disappeared.

We all hurried to get into our armor. Each second that ticked by felt like an hour.

Once we were ready, Maverick commanded us, "Get out there and make as much noise as you can. If we're lucky we'll wake the camp, if we're luckier still the enemy will hear us and call off their attack, but I doubt that will happen."

Just before we left, Fin returned with most of the rest of our House: Ant, Midnight, Tusk, Fennec, Foggy, Princess, Sparrow, and Silence. The last two I didn't want to be here, not in the middle of a fight like this, but I couldn't fault them for coming, the people they loved were in danger.

Maverick told them what to do and we ran in all directions calling out, shouting as loud as we could.

"Alarm!"

"Men in the woods."

"Men behind the camp."

"Watch from all sides."

"Sneak attack!"

That got the camp moving... but it also must have spooked the enemy, or we were just a little too late, as we began to hear the sounds of combat, shouts and cries from all sides; all sides except the direction the enemy should have come, across the battlefield.

The battle had begun.

CHAPTER 23

SPARROW AND SILENCE CAME WITH ME; SHE FLEW OFF TO SEE what she could, while Silence stuck close. He had a longsword and small shield but no armor.

"We had to flee the manor," he said as we moved carefully through the night toward the sounds of fighting. "And we couldn't bring everything. Some brought armor, but I... didn't think I'd need it. I feel a bit stupid about that now." His voice was quavering as we drew closer to the battle-line.

Sparrow returned, flashing back to herself, shaking her head. "My night vision isn't great and the enemies carry no torches, I saw only a shadowy mob of men moving from the forest in to the edges of the camp. Sorry," she said, and I heard the fear in her voice too. She had armor like mine, a breastplate, grieves and bracers, with the addition of a chain skirt to protect her hips and upper legs. She carried a bow and quiver, a short sword at her hip.

What were we doing? I was barely trained for this. Silence was little better. Sparrow was the most experienced but still had never seen true battle like this. She'd always been a scout.

"We... could go back," I said hesitantly. Yet, my *Hero* gift was rising within me, and I needed to be out there. I couldn't run away. I was less concerned about my own death and more about theirs.

You must fight, but you can't bear to see those dearest to you hurt, it's natural. All warriors feel some mix of fear for themselves and their allies. It is what you do now, in this critical moment that counts. Auwei was right.

I saw the momentary relief on Silence's face at my suggestion, but quickly that turned hard. Sparrow's jaw twitched, clenched, determined.

"We stay," Silence said, stalwart and firm.

"We fight," Sparrow echoed his tone.

"We fight to protect this army and... each other," I said. "Stay close if you can."

They nodded to that, then we were moving out, faster now, hurrying to the front.

HAD WE GONE SOUTH OR EAST, THINGS MIGHT HAVE BEEN different. I'll never know. But the North was where the fiercest fighting was that fateful night... and where my true enemies waited.

THE THREE OF US REACHED THE BATTLE LINES AND SUPPORTED the Vauphani troops already fighting, most without armor, some in nothing but nightshirts, fighting without weapons. They'd been caught mostly unawares, sleeping, but they fought fiercely, knowing their lives were on the line.

Silence, Sparrow, and I fought as a unit. Sparrow stayed

behind Silence and me, using her bow to pick off targets coming from the sides. I was quick. Silence was quicker, darting in and out, avoiding the slashes of axes and swords. My spear worked well, I had a longer reach than most of the enemy and dealt with them before they were a threat. But then some strong man caught the haft of the weapon as it was thrust at him. A quick jerk and he pulled it from my hands. Sparrow put an arrow through him a moment later, but I didn't have time to pick up the weapon with others rushing in. I had to switch to swords.

I was surprised to find out how good I was in the chaos of a melee. I would have assumed these dedicated soldiers were well trained, and it isn't that they weren't, but my training seemed to have been... better.

The fighting drew close, the enemy on all sides. Sparrow had thrown down her bow and was using her sword now, the three of us fighting in a tight circle. We may have been better trained, but the sheer number of the enemy wore us down. We all bled from various nicks and cuts, nothing serious... yet.

"I love you... both!" Silence called out.

What was he doing?

I couldn't see him beside me and couldn't spare a glance for fear of an enemy taking advantage of my lapse in attention. But when I heard him grunt in pain, I couldn't help myself.

I looked quickly to see him holding his stomach, shield lost, but he was fighting still. I returned to fighting my foes, but my concern spiked.

He'll not last long with a wound like that, I whimpered internally.

It's a gut wound. He'll last long enough.

Long enough for what? I asked Auwei.

But she had no answer.

Yet it turned out she was right.

A moment later fresh Vauphan troops found us, these ones well-armed and armored. They had probably been at the center of the camp and had time to prepare for the fight. They swept past us, pushing the Elistans back. The three of us were left alone in their wake.

Silence fell to his knees, and Sparrow and I both dropped our weapons to turn and try to catch him as he swayed.

We helped him lay back. His gaze flicked back and forth between us. "I love you," he kept saying.

Spirits no! Don't die you wonderful, innocent man!

I pulled up the light padding under my armor to get a handful of my webbing. "Show me the wound!" I said urgently. He didn't seem to understand, but Sparrow was able to pry his hand away from his belly. I could tell instantly, it had been a stab, not a slash. A small opening, not a long one, but that meant it might also be deep, which seemed likely given how it was gushing blood. I pressed the webbing over the wound, hoping to close and clot it, pressing hard. "Tear up his shirt," I commanded Sparrow. "We need bandages."

"It's filthy."

"It's better than nothing!"

She nodded and began ripping off this shirt and tearing it into strips, tying them together so we could wind it around his mid-section. He lost consciousness, but was still breathing, if shallowly.

I couldn't lose him.

Turning to Sparrow, tears in my eyes and hoarse desperation in my voice I said, "Find Ant, please!"

She nodded and flitted away as a bird a moment later.

Her night sight might not be good, but Ant was massive and hopefully easy to find.

The sounds of battle receded. I hoped that meant the enemy was retreating. I wasn't paying attention, consumed with trying to keep Silence alive as if by force of will alone. He just needed to survive long enough for Ant to get here and heal him, just that long. But time seemed to pull and stretch. Every instant with Silence felt like an eternity. My vision became blurred with tears. The *Hero* gift inside me hardened into a terrible thing fused to revenge. If Silence died, so help the Elistan army. I'd slay them all myself!

Legs! Auwei tried to warn me, but I wasn't listening.

"There she is."

At first, I thought the female voice was Sparrow, leading Ant to me. It was a testament to how addled I was, that it took me far longer than it should to realize two things:

First: that wasn't Sparrow's voice, but I'd heard it before...

Second: there were more than two people drawing close to me. My hairs pricked up and my spider sense detected a group of five, three of them in the forms of large cats.

Pits!

Legs! Move! I listened to Auwei this time.

I ducked and rolled to the side as a clawed hand swept through where I had been. But I couldn't go far, I was surrounded.

Looking up, I saw Lady Claw sneering down at me. Her armor was well fitted showing off her curves, while still remaining practical. She held no weapon, but her hands were gleaming with long claw-like nails. It had been her who'd just tried to kill me.

"I'll gut you and eat your entrails," she said with a feral grin.

How very unpleasant.

The other one in human form was Lynx. His face was hard. I could see a hint of remorse, but far more hatred and fury. He spat out his words when he spoke.

"We got the news of your betrayal just after you left our camp." He clenched his jaw, showing his teeth in a mockery of a grin. "You played me for a fool, trying to sway me while gathering intelligence." He shook his head. "Your House is a menace, and you are the rot at its core!" He held two long curved knives, both nearly the length of a short sword.

I scooped up one of my swords — only one was within arm's reach — and rose, terrified. I may have been able to take Lady Claw and Lynx, but they were not alone. With them was a massive tiger, a powerful lion, and the slinking, deadly form of a jaguar.

I could leap away, out of reach of all of them but Silence would surely die. I knew I wouldn't have time to bend and scoop him up; they were too close. I should have picked him up instead of my sword, but I'd made my choice and now I was stuck. If I left, Silence died. If I stayed, we both died.

My *Hero* gift decided for me. I couldn't leave. Power surged into me, strengthening me as I settled into a fighting stance.

Lady Claw laughed, then lunged at me.

CHAPTER 24

It was a feint. Claw dodged away as I swiped at her. I had hoped to remove one of those deadly, clawed hands of hers, but she was too quick.

The real attack came from Lynx, behind Claw, and Lion behind me. I'd sensed the movement of both of them. I lunged forward, getting in close with Lynx, hoping to avoid Lion. Yet, I only managed to block one of Lynx's long knives, the other blade skittered along the front of my armor, hard enough to leave a gouge, but not hurt me. And I only partially avoided Lion's attack, one of his claws raked over my left calf. I'd shifted enough that the cuts weren't deep, but they were deep enough to bleed and that would cost me strength eventually.

As they retreated, Tiger and Jaguar surged in. Tiger leaped high, while Jaguar kept low. I waited for the perfect instant, then leaped a little while veering into my spider form, with the effect of suspending myself in the air, over Jaguar's slashing claws and under tiger's flashing teeth. They passed by and I returned to my form, lashing out as I did, a glancing blow on Jaguar's hip. The large cat yowled.

I laughed with elation and victory. Five on one and I'd still managed to land a hit. Not a deep one, but enough to celebrate.

Lynx and Claw came at me from different angles, and I spun, going up on one leg to put myself near to sideways, lunging at Lynx, blocking his attack while moving the rest of my body out of his reach, and at the same time kicking Claw's arm.

I then threw myself at Claw, following up with a second, spinning kick and caught her shoulder, sending her to the ground. But I'd ignored the others for just a little too long. I sensed Lion leaping at me while in the middle of my spin kick, I couldn't get out of the way and tried to veer into a spider, but Lion was too quick and caught me mid transition. One set of claws raked along my side, then slammed me — now a spider — down to the ground. I hit hard and three of my spider's legs crumpled under me. Lion leaped away, but the damage was done.

I shifted back to human, feeling the pain in my left leg. I'd not be moving quickly from now on. And his claws had hit behind my armor, my exposed back above my hip, and I felt the burning sting of the four marks upon me.

I tried to move out of the way of Tiger rushing in but put too much weight upon my left leg and fell, crumpling. Tiger hovered over me — massive maw open and heading for my throat — as time seemed to slow.

This was it.

Then a sparrow — shifting into a small woman — hit the side of Tiger's head in full flight and knocked the beast off course, the two of them tumbling to one side.

A charging bull tore through the scene, scoring a glancing blow on Lynx, while Claw nimbly slipped out of his way. She managed a raking claw attack on Maverick's flank. Then my Housemates flooded in to surround me as Ant appeared, kneeling next to Silence. The large man looked at me and my wounds.

"Him first!" I said through gritted teeth and Ant nodded.

I tried to rise, but my leg gave out beneath me, and I cried out despite myself.

Shouldn't I be stronger than this? Shouldn't my gift be helping?

Your gift let you survive five on one for long enough for your friends to arrive. Now let them do some work for a bit.

I conceded that point to Auwei.

Ant gasped, finishing with Silence. I could see the weariness on his features as he turned to me. I wanted to tell him I was fine, to save his strength for fighting, but I couldn't, I was aching and stinging and needed help.

His healing energies flowed through me, my leg strengthening as my cuts shrank, not completely healed, but enough not to bother me too much.

Then Ant winked and drew forth his staff. Yet I saw how he stumbled when he rose. I wondered how many others he'd already healed this night.

I got up, trying to take in everything around me, but in the dark my eyes couldn't catch the movement. It was all too fast. So, I closed my eyes and let my spider-sense take over.

Maverick and Amber were managing to get Tiger to retreat. Jack was attacking Lady Claw, and keeping her at bay. Ant headed for Lion, who was attacking Sparrow. Sparrow herself was a dervish of speed, flitting around the battle even in her human form, dodging the large cat's attacks. I couldn't sense Jaguar, perhaps he'd fled when the reinforcements arrived?

Fennec fought Lynx. Though even as I sensed them, Fennec grunted and went down, Lynx stalking in toward me. That was it for reinforcements from my House, the others must have been elsewhere in the battle and Sparrow had not been able to round them up.

I had one sword in hand and my other was close by. Diving at it, I rolled and came up with both swords before sinking into a fighting stance to face Lynx.

"You've learned a lot of tricks in the short while you've been Bonded," he said, voice heavy with loathing and a hint of weariness. "But I've been Bonded longer, and I know more."

We'd see.

He roared and charged. For a moment, it was all I could do to block his furious attacks, barely able to see his blades in the dark of night. I even closed my eyes, focusing just on what I could feel and centering myself as I defended.

Then I dug in, my gift rising, and I stopped giving ground, holding firm. He roared with frustration as I began to counterattack, seeing the patterns in his swift-bladed style of fighting.

I sensed it, something from him, some intent, before it happened and even as he veered to his avatar, I did the same, doing my leap-evasion from earlier, managing to land on his back as he dove through where I had been. I bit his back, letting all my venom sink into him, but it seemed to do little and he spun his head around raking a tooth over where I was. I jumped away before he hit me. Shifting back to human I slashed at his flank, but he was too quick. He ran a short distance, then turned and roared again, though as a Lynx it came out as a shrieking squeal, not the most intimidating thing, but certainly jarring.

He charged back in and I braced. This time I wouldn't evade. My gift surged, my legs strengthened, arms swelling with power. Again, my senses picked up his intent before it happened. He shifted back to human as he leaped at me, both knives out before him. I saw the opening instantly. Time slowed as I brought my swords together, tight, then as his blades passed to either side of mine, I drove my arms out, causing his blades to go wide of me. But he was still headed straight for me, and seeing his predicament he was veering back into a cat, fangs ready.

But I was inside his guard and just had to time myself right...

...bringing my swords together with all my strength, crossing before me, and severing his head.

The body still hit me with all the force of a leaping, large cat, and knocked me to the ground.

I rolled it off me, blinking blood out of my eyes, as the body twitched and spasmed in the throes of death.

Far too much hot blood covered me. That was a consequence I hadn't entirely been prepared for, but should have expected, cutting a man's head off at close range.

Sparrow appeared next to me.

"You look like The Pits," she gasped, breathing hard.

"I'm aware." I was still trying to get blood out of my eyes. I concentrated on my other sense while I did, but still asked. "How are the others doing?"

"Ant's got Lion under control. Jack's still battling that crazy woman, and Amber and the Boss—"

I heard the cry of pain and felt through my senses the large shape falling to the ground.

Maverick. Though I couldn't tell what had taken him down.

"No!" Sparrow cried out.

I turned, squinting through the blood and tried to peer into the night, but I couldn't see. All I knew was that Amber was now fighting Tiger alone, and he was a big bruiser with speed to boot.

"See if you can do anything for Fennec," I said to Sparrow, remembering how he'd been taken down by Lynx. "I'll help Amber." And I launched myself in her direction.

My vault was more horizontal than vertical, rushing over the ground. I was on track to plunge my swords into Tiger's side... when everything went to The Pits.

I sensed the form only as I drew near. A tiny form, a flying bug of some sort. It moved fast, flying into my path then shifting into a large man, whose fist came up into my gut. Lord War's punch hit me so hard it threw me backwards and my swords were tossed from limp hands.

I landed heavily on my back, skidding in the dirt a few feet, the breath knocked out of me. I gasped but couldn't seem to draw a breath as the massive form of Lord War stalked toward me.

It was only then I recalled his avatar was a warrior wasp.

I was still stunned, frantic for air and unable to move. I couldn't get out of the way as he knelt and slammed his fist into my face.

The bottom of my face crunched, crushed: nose broken, teeth knocked in, my jaw twisted to the side, dislocated. I blacked out—

—and was instantly brought back as pain, unlike anything I'd ever felt before, surged through me and I would have screamed if my broken mouth had been capable. My body convulsed and writhed, out of my control, as my face exploded with pain far beyond the damage already done. Some distant part of me — perhaps Auwei — knew this to be the warrior wasp's sting, one of the most painful things imaginable. But as a man, War's stinger was his fist.

I was distantly aware of Lord War laughing as he slipped

a hand under the collar of my armor to lift me, his fist rearing back for another strike. I'd not survive a second hit.

Then the massive form of a bull hit Lord War, knocking him aside, throwing him. The bull snorted then became a man.

"Spirits," Maverick breathed, kneeling over me. "Ant, we need you now!"

Maverick looked pretty rough himself, bleeding from several wounds, one of his arms held close as if he didn't want to move it much.

"That sting packs quite the wallop, doesn't it? Took me out for a moment." His voice was panicked. "Legs? You in there? Spirits of the... Ant! Hold on, Legs." He smiled as if trying to reassure me, but there were tears in his eyes. "Of all of us, you need to live. You're the one the mistweaver said would ruin all their plans. So you live, you hear me? That's an order!" He looked away. "Bloody bones, War is up again. I gotta go, Ant will be here soon, I promise! You keep fighting!" Then he rose and squared his shoulders. "You want her? You'll have to go through me!"

CHAPTER 25

My world spun, tilting wildly as the shock-inducing pain slowly faded. That left only the broken face pain, which was still enough to make everything hazy.

I'd probably black out again, but I couldn't. I couldn't let Maverick face Lord War alone. Yet all I could do was watch — my spider sense setting the scene — as War charged in. He and Maverick were weaponless, but one hit from those powerful fists of Lord War and he'd sting Maverick, stunning him. That was all he'd need. But Maverick was far from being a hapless bumpkin. His unarmed technique was different from what Amber had taught me, but he was no less skilled and kept batting away War's fists before they could reach him, even managing to land a couple hits of his own on his massive opponent.

Something's happening! Even Auwei's voice seemed far away. She must also be using my spider sense, but was able to sense farther than I could, since I was only barely conscious.

I couldn't talk, but I could still communicate with my True-Bonded. *What?* I asked.

Auwei's voice surged with hope. *Lady Claw is fleeing from Jack.* But just as quickly I felt Auwei's hope turn to despair. *Oh no! It was a feint.*

What?

Jaguar is back! He caught Jack unawares and... Sparrow is trying to stop him, but... he's thrown her off, she's down... and oh! Spirits Alive! Jack's... not moving.

Is Panther going for Sparrow? My heart lurched.

No... Spirits! He's going for Amber. She's having a tough enough time fighting Tiger alone. She's held her own this long, but she won't see Jaguar coming!

Through the haze and the pain, I tried to call out, tried to warn Amber, but all I did was croak a pathetic sound and cause myself more pain. I nearly blacked out. I lost contact with Auwei for a moment, and when I regained enough of myself to speak to her again, I felt her anguish.

Amber?

She's...

No!

Yes.

I heard a roar, a sound so terrifying, so full of primal rage and pain my entire being sought to flee this place.

And I knew who had made that sound.

Ant?

Yes. He's dealt with Lion and is now taking on Jaguar and Tiger alone. Spirits, he's... terrifying...

Wait... someone is arriving... it's... Midnight! She's hurt Lord War. He's fleeing!

Distantly I heard Maverick's weary voice. "I don't know if you can get in there without being hurt yourself, but if you can help Ant, or get him away from those two, Legs needs help!" Then he was kneeling over me again. "One more moment, Legs, Ant is coming." I saw the strained look on

Maverick's face. His forced smile and pained eyes were saying: *by all the Spirits you're a mess.*

Auwei continued her narration of events. *Midnight has joined the other fight. I... yes! Tiger is down, Jaguar is fleeing. He's too fast for Ant to catch. Ant... I think he wants to give chase, but Midnight has stopped him. He's... coming this way. Midnight is flying off, perhaps to make sure Jaguar doesn't circle back once again for a final run at us?*

I saw Ant, face hard, but streaked with tears kneeling over me. I faintly heard him mutter, "At least I can save you." Then I felt his healing pour into me once again, my face mended, the pain faded, but I could see how much it took out of Ant. He'd pushed himself too far. Maverick caught him, laying him down as he passed out. But I was healed.

Take it slow, I can feel how exhausted your body is, all this healing has taken a lot out of you.

Not to mention fighting for my life... and the lives of my friends and family in House Maverick. I sat up slowly, feeling so very weak. My head spun for a long moment, and I breathed a long "ohhh..."

Maverick looked over at me. "You're quite the sight. Who's blood are you covered in?"

After what had happened to my face, probably a lot of my own, but mostly... "Lynx," I groaned.

Maverick smiled. "Good." He got into a crouch and offered a hand to help me up. I took it.

I looked away only for a moment, to get my feet under me, and in that instant the hand holding mine went limp and for the second time that night a hot spray of blood poured over me.

I hadn't been paying attention, hadn't had my senses up. I'd been too tired. I fell back as Maverick released me.

When I looked back, I saw Lady Claw standing behind

Maverick. In one hand she gripped his hair, pulling his head back. Her other hand, claws extended, was a mess of gore from ripping out his throat. She looked a fright, bloody and bruised, eyes filled with madness.

Maverick... was dead, his eyes vacant and unseeing.

It had happened so fast, and I was so weak, I just lay on the ground trembling. My *Hero* gift fled, my spirit shattered at the sight of Maverick's dead eyes and blood-covered body.

"I've killed the head of the House," Claw sneered, voice pained. I could tell she wasn't doing well either. "Now for its heart." She tossed Maverick's corpse to the side as her eyes went hungry with bloodlust.

An arrow caught her a glancing blow on the shoulder and she cried out in shock, looking toward the woods in the distance. She snarled and a moment later was in cat form, bolting away at full speed.

Uncertain what was happening, I knew only that I had to help Maverick. I crawled toward him. Maybe, if I could wake Ant...

But no, Maverick was well dead, far too much blood staining the ground around him. I couldn't believe it. I lost myself, weeping hot bitter tears.

This was my fault. Those Nobles had come to kill me and... and my Housemates had died, protecting me.

Maverick's words came to me, replaying over and over in my mind:

Of all of us, you need to live. You're the one the mistweaver said would ruin all their plans. So you live, you hear me! That's an order!

I needed to live, and for that — for me — how many of my new family had died? Maverick, like a father to me, would never again smile that warm smile of his. Fennec was probably dead. Foggy would never forgive me. Jack had been like an older brother, well more like a stepbrother who thought you were hot and wanted to sleep with you. Ant was alive, but I'd seen the pain written clearly on his face. His words made sense to me now: *At least I can save you*, which meant he hadn't been able to save Amber. She'd been like an older sister to me, more experienced in... everything and always seemingly knowing what I was doing and who I was with. Always there to help. Now she was dead too, and her death had nearly killed Ant.

Spirits! What had I done?

"Legs? What happened?" I recognized the voice, but it took me a long moment to register it.

Alvere knelt, holding me close. "Gods above, this is a mess. What in The Deepest Pits happened here?"

I couldn't answer. If I tried to speak only sobs came out as I cried upon his shoulder.

"Hush. We're here now," he said, stroking my hair. "I found some Fey in the woods. They repaid the fleeing Elistans for their treachery tonight. Then I went looking for you. I saw that woman kill Maverick and come for you. I..." He sighed heavily. "I'm sorry I missed her, but that shot was taken from nearly five hundred yards." I cried harder. "Yes, I know, just..." He held me tighter. "Gods, what a mess," he whispered.

And I couldn't agree more.

A mess that *I* had caused.

CHAPTER 26

I T WAS A LONG TIME BEFORE I COULD DO ANYTHING OTHER than cling to Alvere in desperation and defeat. Wordlessly, he helped me to my feet. I looked around slowly, but there weren't any bodies around me.

"The Fey moved them," Alvere said softly. "Come, you should rest."

"No," I croaked, voice hoarse and raw. "I... I need to see them. I need to know who's..." *still alive and who's dead... who I killed.*

You didn't kill any of them, Auwei said, trying to reason with me, but I wasn't in any mood to listen.

They died for me. That's the same thing. I may not have killed them with my own hands, but I got them killed.

Auwei sighed deeply. She kept trying to send me warmth and love, but I was hollow and cold right now, a void sucking in her emotions without feeling them.

"This way," Alvere said.

I walked, leaning heavily upon him, my legs faltering often, weak as water. Eventually he lifted me into his arms and carried me.

We came to an open area and laid out before us were some of the dead. Of the foes were Lynx, Lion, and Tiger. There were other mundane soldiers, but I gave them little attention.

I sought out those from my House. I found Maverick, Amber, Jack, Fennec, and Tusk. The last must have died elsewhere that night. I stared at them cold and unfeeling for a long moment, as I thanked the Spirits that Sparrow and Silence weren't among the dead.

"Have you seen enough?" Alvere asked, and I could hear the pain and sympathy in his voice.

I took another long moment to paint this picture in my mind. I needed to remember each of these faces. My friends, no my family, who had died for me. Finally, I turned away. Alvere scooped me into his arms once again and carried me to his pavilion. The common area in front had been filled with extra beds and on them lay wounded men.

Alvere set me down at my request as I sought my friends. Silence looked healthy but hadn't yet returned to consciousness. Princess was sleeping, her hands and head were bandaged. Fin looked rough, covered in a lot of bandages, many of which were soaked with blood.

If Fin died, we'd have no way to return home quickly.

"Will he live?" I asked Alvere, knowing the prince had no more information than I did. But a nearby woman, small and pale with dark hair — a Fey — replied to me.

"He will live, though he may be some time in recovering." The small woman seemed to be tending the many wounded in here.

Sparrow looked rough, a bandage on her head, covering one side of her face, and many others on various parts of her. Yet she smiled when she saw me. "I... didn't know what happened to you. I lost consciousness and woke to the Fey tending me." Her smile grew. "I'm so happy you're alive." A tear traced her cheek on the one side of her face not covered by bandages.

I couldn't share her joy. I was happy she was alive, but I was consumed by sorrow over the others who weren't. "Too many died," was my reply to her.

And saying that, I broke down again, falling to my knees and sobbing through my tirade. "They died because of me, died for me. I got them all killed. I'm a curse upon this House. I killed Maverick! He died... I... saw the life go out of him. He was so full of life and now it's gone. How can I ever...?" I babbled some more, incoherent words through my tears. I was lifted to sit up on Sparrow's bed and felt her and Alvere both embracing me, holding me as I blubbered and wept. Yet the pain wouldn't leave me. It was a thorn in my soul, no a thorn was too small, it was a mountain of agony, made of razor-sharp stone, tearing through me.

At some point, I lost consciousness.

I woke in Alvere's bed, but he wasn't with me.

Faint light filtered through the thick canvas. The night had passed.

I rose, still feeling weak.

You should rest, Auwei said.

I ignored her and stumbled out into the common area. Alvere was there, looking tired, speaking to the small Fey woman from the night before. It was she who noticed me first and hushed their conversation, ending it. Alvere came to me.

"You shouldn't be up. Rest."

"I'll rest when I'm dead," I said, voice bitter and harsh.

"There is nothing more to do now," he said.

"There *is* something to do," I spat back. "I'm going to the

Elistan camp. I'll kill them all. You and your army can come with me, or not, I don't care."

Alvere sighed. "My army is in no shape to fight. I have all able-bodied men digging in, building fortifications. We cannot advance and cannot allow them to advance. We must hold here, but we have far too few men." He sighed. "Their attack was a success. Nearly twelve hundred of my men died last night and almost two thousand others are wounded."

He sat me on a nearby cot. I wondered if the person who had occupied this bed had healed or died. In my current mood, and given what Alvere had just said, I presumed they were dead. "The enemy lost roughly six hundred by our count, perhaps more if they took some of their dead with them. And we don't know their wounded. Your Midnight is trying to do some scouting to find out more." He looked down at the thick rug over the earthen floor. Our numbers are roughly even now, and they'll end up with more once all reinforcements arrive. We need to be fortified by then." His voice broke a little. "I don't know what to do, Legs, I..."

I had an answer. "Let me go and kill them all."

"You can't!" he shouted at me. He was at his wits' end too. I knew it, but I had no sympathy for him. I had no feelings at all, only the hollow need for revenge. I needed to hurt something, kill something. "You can't," he said again softly, the bluster having left him. "Please, I can't lose you."

Too late, I was already lost.

No, Legs, you can have your revenge later, when you are healthier and have friends and allies to help you. You have so much to live for! There is love, for Silence and Sparrow and Alvere, and all the others still living of your House! There is the future. You are the one who is going to tear down the corruption within Elista. It won't be today, but you will. It's already been seen. Believe in that. Believe in something. Spirits, you feel so empty. This isn't you!

Yet all I heard of that was: *you feel so empty.*

I am empty, I said to Auwei.

No, you're not, her voice was stern. *You have me inside you at the very least, and I won't let you give up and die!*

I don't want to die. I want to kill. Kill them all. Kill everyone who did this!

No, Legs. Auwei was stern. *I can feel your true emotions. You say you want to kill, but in truth, you want to go into the enemy and thrash about taking some of them with you as you die. You think dying will ease the pain, but all it does is move your pain onto others. And you don't want that. You don't want Silence and Sparrow and the prince to feel what you're feeling now, do you?*

I felt something go hard inside me as I realized the truth of Auwei's words. I *did* want to die. I wanted my death to have meaning, because then *my life* would have meaning. Those who had died would have died for something. And no, I wouldn't wish my current state upon anyone.

But just because I saw the truth, didn't mean I liked it. If I couldn't die, then what could I do? All of what Auwei said earlier was true, there were things that could be done, but not now, perhaps not for some time. And that gaping chasm of time was the emptiness in my soul. An unending abyss into which I fell and fell and fell.

I rose stiffly. "I'll go back to bed then," I said to Alvere, and he smiled. Perhaps he'd thought his words — his love — had swayed me, but they hadn't. I felt hollower than ever. I returned to his room and fell onto the bed. I lay there, unsleeping, unable to rest, staring into the dark void that was my soul.

Days passed.

I was fed and tended to, but otherwise dead to the world.

Alvere and Silence visited me, tried to help with words of encouragement, but I didn't hear them.

Even Auwei tried to lift my spirits. *I never told you the story of Woleia, my first True-Bonded, did I?* she asked, trying to rouse my interest. When I didn't respond, she continued. *I don't like to think of it. There was so much of interest we did together, but all of it was overshadowed by the one great loss in Woleia's life.*

I didn't want to hear about loss right now, so I didn't know why Auwei was telling me this, but I didn't stop her.

There were two men, Andus and Breem, both of whom loved her with all their heart. Auwei hesitated and I could feel her sorrow adding to mine. *But... both wanted her for himself, alone. They weren't willing to share and it tore all three of them apart.*

Again, I didn't want to hear this, but I couldn't block Auwei out.

Please stop, I growled at her.

She ignored me.

Eventually it came to blows. The two of them fought for her. I don't think they would have killed each other, they'd been friends before all of this... but Breem did die in that fight, an accident. He fell and hit his head on a rock. Andus won, but could never forgive himself, and neither could Woleia. They were never together after that.

Great story. I'm feeling so much better. Now be quiet, I grumbled.

You're missing the point, Legs. Auwei gave the sense of a heavy sigh. *You have people who love you, who are willing to share and even work together to give you all the love you deserve. That is the greatest gift in the world and something worth living for. Something to get out of this bed for!*

She was right, but still, I didn't want to hear it. And when

I didn't get up and didn't deign to respond to Auwei she gave up, letting me wallow in peace.

Eventually, Lady Crane came to me, sitting on the edge of my bed.

"You've been sulking long enough," she said sternly, though with a motherly care and concern in her voice. "It is time to get up and rejoin the world. You have duties to attend to."

When I didn't respond, she went on. "The House has met. We talked and decided a few things. Firstly, you should know we've accepted Dove as a member of our House."

Dove... another loved one I'd endangered and who would probably die because of me. I remained stoic, unmoved and unmoving.

"Second, we needed a new head of our House and we've chosen one."

I felt the faintest sliver of curiosity, the only emotion I'd felt in a long time. Still, I lay there, staring at the canvas above me.

"We discussed it for a long time. Neither Midnight nor myself wanted it when..." She sighed heavily. "...when Maverick was chosen, and we still don't."

The man's name sunk like a knife into my heart. I winced.

"Fin is the next most senior member, but he doesn't want the position. He likes being off on his own. He knows he's not a leader. Next would have been Ant." I caught the twitch in her jaw. "He has a good tactical mind, but not a strategic one. He has trouble seeing the big picture at times. And... he... well..." Another sigh. She moved on without finishing her thought. "Foggy's too erratic. Princess too sedate. Dove is too new. Sparrow... well, she agreed with the rest of us on who our leader should be."

By this point, I knew what was coming. A sour sneer crept onto my face.

"We chose you, Legs."

I couldn't help myself, I let out a bitter, harsh laugh. A single "Ha!"

Crane sighed. She let me have my moment of incredulity before she went on. "I don't know how you did it in such a short time, but somehow you've become more to the rest of us than just a Housemate." She laid a hand on my shoulder, giving me a soft squeeze. "Legs, you've become the heart of this House, and now we want you to be its head as well."

Those words — echoing what Lady Claw had said after ripping out Maverick's throat — drove a spike of pain and fury into my heart. I sat up as an indignant rage flared to life within me.

"You're all bleeding mad!" I yelled at Crane, and she flinched back at the vehemence of my vicious words.

At that, the flap to my room was pushed aside and Silence and Sparrow entered. Sparrow limped, leaning on Silence, still covered in bandages and looking weak. Wordlessly they came to me sitting to either side of me, hugging me without shame or pity, just the purity of their love.

Behind them, the rest of the House filed into the small room. Next was Dove, beautiful and resplendent in white, as usual. She sat on the bed close to me. Then Fin, still in bandages and looking like he could barely walk. Ant, looking like he'd lost some of his massive muscle, drawn and fatigued. I wondered how much he'd been helping with the healing. Midnight, grim but stalwart and sure, green eyes blazing with intensity, drilling deep into my soul and shining a light in the darkness there. Foggy, drawn and sad — he'd lost his brother and they'd been so very close — but with a determined quirk of a smile on his face. Princess, with the ferocity of a hunting cat in her golden eyes.

Behind them all, peering in without entering, was Alvere. He wasn't a part of the House, but I saw the immensity of his love for me in those brilliant blue eyes. He smiled and nodded as my family of Housemates drew close around me.

"I believe in you," Crane said with certainty in her voice.

"I believe in you." The words were echoed by the others:

Ant's deep baritone...

Foggy's high tenor...

Princess' soft silken tones...

Fin's full base...

Midnight whispered the words, but her tone was sure. "We believe in you."

Dove smiled. "I've always believed in you and known you'd do great things."

Sparrow kissed my left cheek and breathed close to my ear. "I love you, and I believe in you."

Silence kissed my right cheek and whispered, "I *need* you, Legs. I believe in you and need you to believe in yourself."

I believe in you, Auwei said firmly within me.

And the outpouring of love and esteem from my family finally broke the armored dam I'd built around my soul. All the emotions I'd been repressing flowed out. I felt an immensity of grief for those I'd lost, as well as my wonderous love for Silence, Sparrow, Alvere, and my family. So much pain and sorrow, but also a heartfelt joy. I was alive and so many I loved were still here with me.

I broke down and wept for a long time as my family drew closer around me, hands outstretched to touch me if they couldn't get close enough to hold me.

I let out all the pent-up filth I'd been clinging to. I'd wanted to wallow in the agony of loss, the pain of what I felt I'd caused. I couldn't quite let it all go. I still blamed myself for far too much of what had happened, and rightfully so. If I'd never joined Maverick House, most of what they had gone through would not have happened. If I'd died in that first attack by the mistweaver the nation would have left Maverick alone.

But I couldn't deny that what we had done was right, was just, was good. And if Elista was to see the error of its ways it would need Maverick House to show it.

No, not Maverick House anymore.

Legs House?

Spirits, that sounded silly. I actually laughed in the middle of my heavy tears and several of the group moved back a bit. I managed to get ahold of myself long enough to mutter through my tears, "You all win. But by the Spirits, we can't call it Legs House."

Others chuckled a little as well.

"What would you suggest?" Crane asked.

We would be the House that crawled, unexpected, under the feet of the nation of Elista. We'd bring them down, even though we were small, and almost broken.

We were: "House Spider," I said firmly.

And with that I accepted my position... and my fate.

Don't miss the next book in the series!

FORM AND FURY
The Mists of Elista Trilogy, Book Three

End a war and stop the cabal of Nobles who are destroying my country? Yeah... I can do that

War sucks. I've lost friends who were like family to me. So, I'll end this war, if it's the last thing I do. And with an entire nation hunting me... it just might be.

At least I still have my lovers, and the "Loving Legs" club might even be open to new members. These amazing paramours of mine, along with what remains of my misfit noble house are all that are keeping me sane. Because really, what chance do I have against mistweavers, madmen, and warmongers?

And when one plan after another goes awry, it seems like I'll never succeed. It's only with love and sacrifice I'm going to win this war. I just hope I won't have to sacrifice what I love.

OTHER BOOKS BY CLARA WILS

THE GRECIAN GODDESS TRILOGY

written with Tessa Cole

Kiss of the Goddess, book 1

Power of the Goddess, book 2

Bonds of the Goddess, book 3

THE MISTS OF ELISTA

Bonds and Blood, book 1

Shape and Shadows, book 2

Form and Fury, book 3

SHADOWS OVER ELISTA

Double Discovery, book 1

Double Danger, book 2

Double Disaster, book 3

Double Doom, book 4

Double Destiny, book 5

SECRETS GODS KEEP

written with Tessa Cole

Craving Demons, book 1

Chaos Demons, book 2

Claiming Demons, book 3